Fiction In Red II ™

AIRLINE EDITION

by Eddy Ivy™

Fiction in Red II
Airline Edition
All Rights Reserved.
Copyright © 2013 Eddy Ivy
v4.0

Cover Illustration and Design by: Fiona McAuliffe

Eddy Ivy Press

ISBN: 978-0-9822684-1-4

Library of Congress Control Number: 2009924103

PRINTED IN THE UNITED STATES OF AMERICA

Foreword

There are a collection of 25 off the wall short stories in this book. In order to enhance your reading experience a twist has been added. All of the words of this book which are in red lettering are fictional. These tales impart wisdom, promote intellect, evoke fantasies, enhance vocabulary, provide entertainment and install morals.

Special thanks to the following individuals.

Fiona McAuliffe, The cover artist who made my dream a reality.

Bonnie Darves, Author, writer, for editing services.

Contents

1
Maui Cruiser

My junior year of college in Ashland, Oregon, was painfully short and packed. Between working 30 hours a week at Pizza Shack and running on the cross-country team—not to mention carrying a technical "full load" of 13 credit hours—when the spring term ended I was ready for a break from reality.

Joe, one of my buddies on the team, was from Maui, Hawaii. During spring break he had come home with me to Oregon's Bay Area, as most schools closed their dorms at that time. My parents were always full of surprises, and since they knew that I was bringing home a guest, this visit was to be no exception. On the table when we arrived were two round-trip "red-eye" tickets to Florida, for a flight departing out of Portland 32 hours later.

We were on our way to Daytona Beach, Florida, and then on to Sarasota! It was a good thing that my parents had left the phone number of my dad's friend, Rex, where they would be staying, or we would have been lost. After that adventure, Joe and I became pretty good friends. So it was no surprise, actually, when he offered to let me come over and stay with him on Maui for part of the summer.

After finals were over I had three weeks to plan for the trip and make arrangements for my senior year. Joe's schedule, however, was much more **stringent**. He had less than a week to be packed and in the air since he lived in the college dormitory. Selling the idea to my parents to spend their vacation in Hawaii was another huge hurdle to overcome. OK, not really, I must admit!

It is nice when you plan things out well. I finished my finals, made arrangements to come back to the pizza place as an on-call delivery driver, secured a rental agreement with my landlord, Sherm, for the following school year, and stashed my **sundries** in a storage unit. The extra three weeks I stayed in Ashland helped fill my unusually skimpy **coffers** for the seven-week trip ahead, as I was able to pick up loads of overtime at Pizza Shack.

My next task was to pack for my Hawaiian Island trip, it took about ten minutes. My list included two pair each of running shoes, shorts, socks, and T shirts and my **Dopp** kit. This left just enough room for all of my scuba gear, minus my air tanks. Interestingly, my parents had decided to spend a week in Honolulu prior to my coming over, so the plan was to meet up with them for about a week. Then I would hop a Cessna to Maui.

Fiction in Red II

On my arrival at my parents' rented condo, my mom went into a fit. She had opened my suitcase and exclaimed, "Eddy, where are your clothes?" Half laughing, I replied, "Gee, Mom! This is Hawaii. Who needs clothes!" Within a few hours I soon had a new wardrobe of Hawaiian shirts and a few new pairs of pants for the next school year. I suppose I couldn't have planned that one any better!

That week flew by, and I soon found myself at Joe's place. The very first evening I discovered what it was like to live a laid-back lifestyle. I was out on the **veranda** reading the local tabloid when an ad jumped out at me. It read, simply: Maui Cruiser -- $200. My parents had been paying 50 bucks a day for their car and 20 bucks for a couple days of my scooterized **escapade**s—and the thought of paying such exorbitant prices bugged me immensely.

The realization that I only had a $500 limit on my student VISA card started to push my laid-back brain into overdrive. I called the guy up who had placed the ad, and learned that the "cruiser" had a new brake job and new tires, but he was leaving for the mainland and had to unload the vehicle.

When I asked him when I could look at it, he let it slip that he was leaving on a plane the next morning. "The sooner, the better," he said. The vehicle was only three miles away, so Joe and I used the trick of leap-frogging on his bike to make the journey. He would ride a block as fast as he could, stop, get off, and then start running. I would then pick up the bike as soon as I got to it, and ride as fast as I could for about a block past him. Then we'd start the process over again.

Arriving at the shack where the seller lived, I saw what I thought was a thing of beauty: a 1976 Volkswagen Thing. It really complemented the dive it sat next to. The owner, Dave, ambled out while I was inspecting it. Shaking his hand, I asked to take it for a test drive.

After he instructed me that the doors didn't work, I deduced that it was a good thing that the canvas convertible top was long gone. After hopping into the car we were off. I was surprised how well it shifted and handled, and decided after a couple of miles that it was mechanically sound despite the rust and overall excessive wear. It would be well worth $200, and would easily last a month, if not a couple of years! Turning around and heading for Dave's dive, I pulled it into the driveway.

When we parked the vehicle in front of the shack, I asked if the car had any problems that I would need to think about. "Well, it burns about a quart of oil a week, Eddy," he divulged. "But I have all of the new parts and repair receipts here, which add up to over $700—and that's not counting the new brakes and tires I bought just last month." I looked at the receipts and checked off what had been replaced and repaired. Then I borrowed a flashlight and realized that he was probably telling the truth. The rotor cap, coil and plug wires were all brand new; everything looked in astoundingly good order.

Fiction in Red II

Then, surprising Joe and myself to a point, I offered Dave the following "$100 right now, or $50 at the airport." He replied, "Dude! The tires alone cost me over $100!"

"I understand," I replied. "But what are you going to do tomorrow, leave the keys in the ignition? Besides, the engine is going to blow any day if it's burning that much oil; and how many offers have you had on this rust bucket?"

Without giving him a chance to **retort**, I kept my "rap" going. "Think about it! You can see the pavement through the passenger's side floorboard, and it doesn't have a top anymore, Dave. Even Fred Flintstone wouldn't drive this thing!" I pronounced.

It worked! I handed him $100 in twenties, took a signed-off title (there was a whole year left on the tags!), and my transportation problem was solved. On the way home, Joe asked, "If the engine's going to blow, why did you buy it?"

I explained that the only engine I really knew a lot about was in this car, because it was the same one used in most of the sand buggies driven in Oregon. "In the last eight years I've taken apart at least a dozen of these exact engines and then put them back together," I said. "Besides, it's almost a brand-new engine." I added that the car hadn't smoked a bit on the test drive and I had noticed there were huge oil puddles all over the dirt driveway when we drove up. When I had inspected underneath I had noticed that the only mechanical problem appeared to be a few missing bolts on the oil pan along with a few fresh beads of oil where the missing bolts should have been.

Tapping the oil gauge, I said, "I'm surprised there's enough oil pressure to move this thing after a couple of days of oil loss!"

My friend said, "No way, Dude." I offered to prove my point, by taking an old gallon milk container and placing it where the drips are coming out--and then checking it in the morning. Sure enough, by the next morning about a dixie cup of oil had **decidedly** made its way out of the oil pan. All I had to do was drain the oil, replace the seal and tighten it up. Hopping over the doors and into the Thing, Joe and I were off to the local auto parts store. I bought four quarts of oil, five bolts, a new oil pan seal and a new oil filter for luck. Within a couple of hours my car was pronounced mechanically sound after I dropped Joe off at work.

Joe was working days at one of those exclusive tourist restaurants, so I was on my own. It was probably a good thing that I had a **mullet** at that time, because it made me look like a local, and therefore didn't run into any major problems with any of the "real" locals. Of course, there were always extra beers in a cooler if I was at a beach--and I was more interested in snorkeling and diving than in surfing on someone else's "turf" anyway.

I learned a lot that first week about the native culture and traditions. Joe and his cousins lived off the land much of the time, in their **meanderings** around the island. Soon I was eating many types of seaweed, raw **mussels** off the beach, Chinese hats, raw fish, breadfruits, guavas, and generally anything that Joe's extended family would eat first, of course!

The second weekend we went to the Seven Sacred Pools on the road to Hana. This winding road takes several hours to navigate. It is an achievement of insanity, as it is carved out of the sides of cliffs over the sea. It's also bumpy, too well traveled, and yet still passable. Stopping for wild breadfruit and guavas we eventually made it to our destination.

The seven main pools are situated in an area that is an interesting **aberration** of nature, in that they are formed from solid rock. They are all connected by a stream flowing through each one. Their uniqueness is in the way they are fed. At the edge of each one, the stream flows over the lowest part of the edge into the next one. This stately stair stepping configuration makes for a majestic array of waterfalls which vary in height from 25 to 45 feet.

The biggest problem for tourists who want to experience the view of these wonder-falls is that they are located in a canyon accessible only from the beach or the bridge, which is located over the middle of the chain of falls. I learned that the locals jump off the bridge, just for the fun of it. Anxious to check out the scene, I asked Joe if that was why we were there. Joe's cousin said, "Hey, for a **Houlie**, you're pretty perceptive, Eddy."

Going out to the middle of the bridge, I said, "You have got to be kidding me. That is at least an 80-foot drop!" Joe gave me the particulars. "First, Eddy, do you see this little red cross over here? That's the precise spot where you have to stand when you jump," he said, "or else you will hit the canyon walls when you go down."

I looked down again; adding to the exhilaration of the upcoming jump was the up-**sheering** structure of the canyon itself. From each end of the bridge's span the **ramparts** appear to **converge** like a pair of scissors blades held upright and opened at a 10-degree angle.

Holding my right hand down over the railing about a foot away from the red cross, I realized that Joe was probably right. On either side of the red cross, moving my hand a foot in either direction, I wasn't able to see the water on both sides of my hand. I wondered how many people had wound up **ricocheting** off the walls.

Just for kicks, I asked, "How wide it is from side to side at the bottom?" Joe said it was "about eight feet." I then asked what else I ought to know, besides that I should go in feet first and align myself straight up before tensing every muscle in my body just before I impact. And also, "by the way, how deep is the pool?"

Eyeing me soberly, Joe said there are a few more things you should know. "It's about 10 feet deep, and it is possible to hit the bottom, so you should only bend your knees in that split second after you are completely under the water but before you hit the bottom," he said with a smirk. "The **optical illusion** of the sheen speeding by creates a euphoric state. This altered reality causes a lot of people lose their balance, so focus on the water Eddy."

At this point I didn't say anything except, "You two go first." Joe stood up, made his Catholic sign of the cross, and took the plunge, as did his cousin. I, on the other hand, recited the entire Lord's Prayer, and realized that the Seven Sacred Pools no longer pertained to Hawaiian legends, but rather to young men with too much **testosterone** who were willing to potentially sacrifice everything for a cheap thrill.

What they hadn't told me was that the only way out of the canyon was to make three more jumps. They had been quick to make it to the next one as soon as I had hit. Unfortunately, I had to leave my prescription glasses in the glove compartment of the "Thing." Following my companions as fast as I could, they nonetheless asked why I was going so slowly. When I replied that I didn't want to hit any rocks when I made the jumps, they must have simultaneously realized that I obviously couldn't see very well without my glasses. Looking at each other they said, "Oh, OK. That makes sense."

A couple of days later, having survived the big dive, I showed up at Joe's house with the catch of the day. It cost only $2 for a tank of air, and Joe's Hawaiian sling for spearing fish, which had made for some darn good fishing. From then on fresh fish was on the menu every night. I don't think Joe's parents wanted me to leave after that second week. His dad jokingly announced that he hadn't eaten that well since he was single. Their two extremely fat cats purred and silently agreed.

Later that night, I went out to the Thing and brought in a 100-foot climbing rope. Taking it to the back porch, I had started to inspect it intently on the railing of their deck while waiting for my tea to brew. In the tone and quizzical way that only Joe can come across with, he asked "Dude! What in the world did you buy that for?" I told him that I hadn't purchased it, but that the seller had forgotten to take the rope, along with about $900 worth of other climbing gear, out of the trunk, probably due to the fact that the lock on it was broken, just like the front doors.

"So what are you doing with it now?" he asked. I told him that although I had only been scuba diving in the area for a couple of weeks, I had discovered a treasure that I want to go after. Squinting up his eyes in a puzzled **configuration**, he gave me a this-is-going-to-be-a-good-one look, and then stared at me like I was nuts.

"You mean, like, pirate's gold, Eddy?" he stated in a **mocking** voice while raising two fingers on each hand to indicate quotation marks.

I laughed so hard that I almost spilled my tea, and said, "Remember when I put my glasses away at the seven pools?"

Joe nodded. "I've noticed," I started, "that most people make the same mistakes all over the world—and over the last 10 years I've been finding tons of goodies where people **collide** with water." It doesn't matter, I explained, whether the jumpers were heading off a dock, a bridge or a ledge. "As long as there is a spot where people are making contact with water," I continued, "There will be sunglasses, coins, watches and who knows what else."

Still in disbelief, I further supported my little theory by reminding him to think about how many people he had seen jump off of the Seven Sacred Pools Bridge, and asked, "So how many people have you seen below that bridge, wearing scuba gear?"

Visibly excited, all he said was, "I want half, Eddy!"

That very night we began the preparations for our adventure to go where, so to speak, no one had gone before. A proper well-thought-out plan would be **crucial**, I knew, if we were to successfully execute our dangerous treasure hunt. Scuba tanks hold 3,000 PSI (pounds per square inch) of air, and I did not want to find out what would happen to one if it were dropped from a height of 80 feet. Likewise, we had more than the bridge drop to consider; there were three other drops we had to think about as well.

The first problem to solve was how to devise a braking mechanism off of the bridge for the rope. The best thing we could come up with was a loop brake. I didn't want to degrade the climbing rope by exposing it to the friction and excessive wear of direct contact with the bridge's concrete rail. After all, I knew that it was a professional climber's rope with a price tag of more than $180 new.

To avoid excessive rasping of my rope, I decided to thread it through an old nylon reinforced garden hose. In a **mock** simulation, we tested the plan of looping it over, and through around the handrail of Joe's wooden deck. Surprisingly, it only took one loop to provide adequate braking for our 45-pound air tanks.

The second problem was the next three waterfall drop-offs. I had previously spotted a yellow two-man raft next to their backyard pool. By lowering our gear to the lower pools in rafts, I reasoned, we would add an extra measure of protection. I asked Joe what he thought about securing our gear in the raft with bungee cords attached to the safety rope handles. **Snidely** shaking his head, he said, "You're either insane or a genius, Eddy. But how do you propose we get the rafts down?"

I had to admit that the idea wasn't something I'd attempted before, but I proposed the specifics. "We just tie a weight belt to one end of our 40-foot rope, and secure the other end to the front of the raft. On the back of the raft we will tie the last remaining 24 foot long piece of rope with a loop tied in the end. Then we'll lower the contraption by threading the 100-foot rope through the loop to the 50 foot mark. Next we will lower it until we are out of slack and then let go of one end of the rope," I explained. "It should survive the resulting six-foot drop. And yes, we will make sure to tie off one end of the 100 foot rope to the bridge!"

That "weekend" we loaded up and were ready to go early in the morning, which, given that it was Hawaii, was Monday morning at 10 a.m. The trip was slow and **arduous** as usual, and if you ever make the trip along the Hana Highway, you will find out why. At our destination we used duct tape to cover the little red cross with a sign proclaiming: DIVERS BELOW! Please wait until cleared before jumping!

The announcement worked well as it wasn't the busy season and the normal weekend crowd wasn't there. At any rate only a few seasoned jumpers were on site, and they appeared to be leaving anyway. They admitted what we already knew: That doing that dive once or twice in a day is usually enough of a thrill for anyone!

The few people that were already at the sacred pools came over to the bridge and asked us if we were professionals. "We're both certified through NAUI" (National Association of Underwater Instructors) I replied. Then we prayed under our breath that nothing would go wrong!

The plan worked perfectly. The rubber raft landed upright and the tanks stayed secure. Joe was able to maneuver the raft upstream by swinging the rope back and forth by using the dive belt "anchors" as pendulum ballasts before it touched the top of the water. The last things we lowered were our masks, fins, snorkels, dive knives, gloves, booties, and a crow bar--just in case we found a treasure chest.

As the water level in the pools is relatively shallow on average, measuring 12 feet deep at the most, we had a lot of scuba air time to explore the bridges' main pool. However, we had only two tanks between us, and we had decided beforehand to use our snorkels and face-masks to scope out the bottom before committing to use them. It turned out that the bottom was composed of sand, gravel, and to a lesser extent, a thin film of mud and algae. What we weren't ready for were the two wedding rings, three wedding bands, eight watches, hundreds of coins and the mother lode--a very nice Rolex watch! We couldn't believe it, and were stoked to put the tanks on.

At that point a few people wanted to make the jump. We gave them the high sign, and decided to tell anyone who asked that we were just looking for a watch we had lost the week before. The stream was actually a bigger help than we had anticipated. When we finally started to troll for treasure side by side, we started on the downstream side. The slow-moving current helped keep our line of visibility relatively clear while we combed through the muck.

When we were finally out of air our treasure chest had accumulated in size to that of a large cigar box. We filled up the rubber rafts, and once again our plan of descending over the remaining falls worked flawlessly. The trip home was punctuated by our unending bursts of exhilaration. We were anxious to get home and share the story of our adventure.

Fiction in Red II

At dinner that night, Joe's dad joked that he had lost a Rolex there once, and we both laughed snidely. That night was a ceaseless round of laughter and jokes that I sure wish I could remember now. The celebratory atmosphere, looking back, not only capped the exciting day but cemented it in my memory.

The next day we went to see a local jeweler who, we were told, bought scrap gold and jewelry at market values. When we dumped the contents out on the table, he stared at us warily as if we had broken into someone's home and stolen the family jewelry box! He asked accusingly, "Fellas, where did you get all of this stuff?" When we recounted our tale he started to laugh, and said, "I've actually been expecting you guys. I got a phone call from your dad a few minutes ago, Joe." The Rolex was the real thing and the scrap gold weighed in at over two ounces. Only one small diamond out of the three rings was real, but we were **ecstatic** when we pocketed the $1,100 check. This trip was turning out to be the best vacation ever!

I was understandably sad when my six weeks in paradise came to an end. I decided to buy an extra couple of suitcases for the trip home, as I had purchased a few luxury items that I normally wouldn't have had the funds for.

The last order of business was to unload the Thing, the contraption that had made my odyssey to Maui a great success. I hatched an idea.

Eddy Ivy

"Hey, Joe. Since you don't have a car, how about buying mine for, say, $200?" Joe put his hand to his chin, feigned being deep in thought, and replied, "Well, Eddy. How about $50 dollars, at the airport?"

What a bargain!

Morals of the story:

1. *Look before you leap!*

2. *Think before you leap!*

3. *A fool and his possessions are soon parted!*

4. *Intellectual visualization is an underutilized tool.*

5. *People are pretty much the same world-wide.*

6. *Take advantage of golden opportunities.*

7. *Learn from other peoples mistakes.*

8. *Fathom it before you fathom it.*

9. *If it's dangerous, ask as many questions as you possibly can.*

2
Miss America

When you listen hard you can almost hear the written **lyrics**, which remind us that there is a time for everything under the sun. If you are like most people, there are things in your life that you wish you hadn't said. Once, while talking with a junior high student I didn't know very well in my 8th grade class, I made the mistake of boasting that I was the toughest kid in school. I had been transferred into this new school about three months earlier and felt pretty confident that I knew everyone well enough to make this statement. Little did I know that Jimmy considered himself the school's official fight coordinator.

In fact, within minutes of our conversation's conclusion, Jimmy had led me into a confrontation that I had no idea was going to take place the next day. While walking to my metal shop **fabrication** class, the only thing on my mind was a required welding project. Without warning, someone grabbed me from behind and pushed me up against a glass wall and hit me twice in the head. It was Tracy, another wrestler I had come up against in meets when I was attending my previous school. Screaming loud enough for the rather large group of people rounded up in advance to witness this display, he cried out, "So you think you're the toughest guy in school?"

Keeping my cool and sizing up the situation, the realization hit me that all I needed to do was to lift up one of my arms to break his grip (or worse, if you know anything about martial arts). As Tracy already had been involved in several other scuffles, I knew that he was now headed for expulsion. But that wasn't the problem at hand.

Stopping to think wasn't an option at the moment, since he decided to hit me in the face two more times. Using the only tools at my disposal, the words came out as follows: "If we get into it here, Tracy, you know as well as I do that we're going to end up breaking out all of the glass in this floor to ceiling wall over to our right--and that everybody within 20 feet will be cut up and injured."

Watching more than 100 people scrambling and falling backwards over themselves from my spoken words was quite **gratifying**. As no one picked up on the reference, or understood what I had just done, my next words were, "Why don't we go outside, where no one will get hurt?" Loosening his grip, he let me lead the next 50 feet to the back door. This was going to be the first fight I had ever run away from.

As my feet reached the pavement outside the door, I sprinted out back and around the gym, only to come close to running straight into the principal. Evidently, Mr. Wordsmith had been misinformed on purpose that there was going to be a fight on the lower football field. This was, of course, the opposite side of the school where the actual fight had been scheduled by my unknown foes.

My involvement in this one-sided confrontation was **generic** in nature, so no punishment was levied against me except a warning. However, both the official fight coordinator and the toughest guy in school were expelled. For the good of all, I might add.

Years later, in 1982, I found myself in a much worse situation. One night I was alone in a bad section of Chicago, and it was an eye-opener, truly. A few of my buddies had decided to abandon me as a joke while I was using the rest room. Realizing what had happened, the natural response was to walk outside and try to hail a cab.

Life doesn't always go according to plan, though, when the locals decide to have some fun with you. Herding me into a side alley, a small group of young men decided to use me as a punching bag. After receiving what felt like hundreds of kicks and punches, the feel of the ground was comforting, since that meant only three sides of my body were being pummeled.

Holding my hand over my head and the other over my kidneys, an idea came to me straight away. Loudly screaming, out came the words, "Why don't you let me get up and fight like a man?" Yes, the suckers fell for it--hook, line and sinker.

Standing up slowly, I chose two victims. Taking one step forward and then planting both feet on the ground I jumped up, while grabbing by the hair the two men blocking my passage to the street. Using them as leverage to exit, and running as if my life depended on it, I found relative security by weaving in and out of moving traffic, which caused quite a stir.

When I finally made it to the sidewalk, after running over a mile I was stopped by a street cop. Bleeding and in bad shape, the authorities who came to my aid called for an ambulance, as I had no clue where I was or who my assailants were, on account of the blackness of the night. Thus, my recovery began in the **trauma** section of a very expensive hospital. It was not exactly the adventure I had planned and was going to last two months instead of a few weeks.

Six weeks of physical therapy in a hospital can really wear on you, but the nurses and doctors were very thorough in my treatment regime and weren't going for my idea of getting out of the place. Their job, as they reminded me countless times, was to make sure that I was well--no exceptions.

The day before my scheduled release, I had been allowed to go swimming, as a part of my recovery therapy. Returning to my wing, the sight of a crowd gathered around a cute dark-haired woman about my age caught my attention. I asked the nurse what was going on, and she replied that the **reigning** Miss America was visiting.

Moving in closer to get a better look, I kidded myself that she was an eight--maybe even a nine--on a scale of one to ten, as I still really didn't believe that she was the **venerated** person I'd been told she was. After a formal introduction to the growing crowd, it was announced that a brief question-and-answer session would take place. No one else appeared willing to seize the moment, so I decided to go for it.

Raising my hand, I said, "Miss Elizabeth, I've got a couple of questions." With a nervous smile, she gazed at me, and said, with a lovely laugh in her voice, "Why, sure." When I blurted out, "Are you a Christian? And may I kiss you?" I could tell that those were probably the last two questions she would possibly have expected. However, in the span of time it takes for a person to smile, she propelled herself from a nine into a 1,000, in what, to this day, was the most incredible transformation I have ever witnessed. Immediately, everyone in the room understood, without question, why she was Miss America.

When she said "yes," and "yes" again, my beaming smile surely showed my **elation**—or something very close to it. Walking from the back of the crowd, still bruised but fully recovered I stepped up, and out of respect, gave her a soft,

loving and not particularly lingering kiss on her left cheek—
an experience I will never forget. She smiled sweetly, as the
cameras clicked away, preserving the shining moment for
eternity.

*Moral of the story: Throughout life, there will be times to run
and times to fight; however, the most important judgment
call you will ever have to make is following through with
your faith and convictions.*

3
Money

If you've ever waited tables you know that breakfast tips are generally terrible. Paradise Lodge, the main restaurant on Mount Rainier, is no exception. One particularly slow morning on the eastern side of the restaurant, the sun was just breaking over the horizon. As the summer light flooded through the windows and across the room, the bright **ambiance** made me long to be outside enjoying the fresh air.

The combination of those invitingly warm rays, the lack of **patronage**, and the spectacular views of colorful meadows, underscored by my love of hiking around the treeline of majestic Mount Rainier, was making my normally erect shoulders droop and professional **demeanor** slack. My duties as a waiter had all but vanished. **Unbeknownst** to me, that was about to change.

Four elderly women came in just under the wire arriving seconds before the 9 am cutoff. Flustered, they sputtered that they had overslept in their rooms upstairs and had been awakened, divinely, by the aromas of bacon and eggs frying.

Upon hearing that, their pleas of "may we please have breakfast?" and "we promise to be quick" had worked in their favor, I muttered under my breath **facetiously**, "Gee, thanks, Chef."

The patrons sat down in my area, which on that morning was a territory of six large round tables **situated** in front of the towering, almost bay-like windows. Greeting them with a smile that took some real effort on my part to produce, I handed them menus and asked if they would like coffee. In **unison**, the women flipped over their coffee mugs from their classic upside down restaurant position. Giving them my biggest smile, this one genuine, and emitting a silent exhale chuckle, I **deduced**, "So you're all sisters, I presume?" One said, "You're very perceptive, and by the way, we want the real stuff." With caffeine? I queried, in a cheery upbeat tone. By this time, my mood was steadily improving.

After we'd gone through the pleasantries and going out of my way to ensure that I had gotten their orders right, I summed them up as roughly spanning the 73-to-80 age range, being very well to do and very down to earth, and not stuck up in the slightest. All of which was giving me a wider **berth** to have some fun.

As I walked back to the kitchen, I mentally noted the facts. These dames were laid back, no Queen's English, and if not perfectly **prim,** proper nonetheless. They were nicely attired in well-made clothing, and their shoes, crafted in a sturdy **patent leather,** were spotless and recently shined.

Fiction in Red II

Two of the women wore elaborately hand-crafted **brooches** made from white gold. The two nearly identical pieces were shaped like butterflies encrusted with diamond crystals along the four wings. The noteworthiness of these pieces was that the central bodies of the butterflies were composed of five half-carat diamonds, and on the outer tip of each of the four outer wings was a single half-carat diamond. Despite their ornate design, the pieces didn't appear the least bit **gaudy** while worn on the womenfolk's out-of-fashion all-wool blazers. Interestingly, all four wore plain gold wedding bands, but none of the rings featured traditional diamond mountings.

Making my way back from the kitchen, I carried a pot of the good stuff, freshly made and extremely hot, along with a silver creamer that I had filled out of consideration. I had forgotten to ask the ladies if they'd like cream, but I wanted to err on the side of caution as I didn't want to appear unprofessional. Coming out with the best service we had seemed to be appropriate even though they were basically the last customers in the lodge.

As I poured the first cup of coffee, the lady whose cup I was filling exclaimed, "Money!" Her **shrill** voice filled the lodge, and I was not only **taken back** but in a mild state of shock. Then, as fast as an 80-year-old woman can physically move, she took her teaspoon and scooped out some of the coffee. I looked at her and then at her sisters quizzically, and ventured, "OK, did I miss something here? What just happened?"

Eddy Ivy

They all laughed, in a tinkling unison, and the lady who scooped out the coffee said, matter-of-factly: "When we were in our teens, it was the Great Depression, and our family was very **impoverished**. As an example, we couldn't afford sugar or cream. But we actually sold our rights to buy a 10-pound bag of sugar to people who actually had enough money to buy it, just so that we could afford the luxury of plain coffee. One of the things our mother did to instill hope in us was to go through a little ritual. She would say that if, after your coffee was freshly poured, you were quick enough to lift up your spoon from the table and scoop out the **inevitable** bubbles from the center of the cup and into your mouth, before they made their way to the edge of the cup, you were then going to come into some money very soon."

I smiled and returned every few minutes to fill their cups, sensing that I was the one who had somehow come into riches, at a most unexpected time. Now that was a nice tip!

Moral of the story: In the long run, words of wisdom are always better than money.

4
Montana State Nursery Surprise

I t was Thursday afternoon the day before my seventh-grade term project was due. The assignment itself was easy; my problem was that I hadn't even started on it. We were to collect 25 flowers, 15 wild and 10 domestic, and then mount the blooms with tape on construction paper, labeling them with both their common names and their scientific names, **genus** and **species**.

My grandparents owned and operated the Montana State Nursery, and that is why, as you might well imagine, I had such a **lackadaisical** attitude toward the assignment. I had four things that most of my classmates didn't: hundreds of wild and domestic flower species around my house, a forest for a back yard, the experience of having spent many hours in the Montana State Nursery two states away, and, most important, an impressively large library of my grandmother's flower books at home.

Just before he let out our class that day, our science teacher, John decided to make a last-minute announcement.

He said that the student who included the most flowers in his or her project would earn 50 points of extra credit for the semester. Wow, I thought, that would be exactly enough to get me an A instead of a B for the class!

Hopping off the school bus, I raced straight into the library in our daylight basement. I walked into the attached garage and grabbed a couple of sawhorses and a piece of plywood to construct a makeshift project table. This would give me a means of housing the anticipated pile of petals I would soon collect. Then I pulled nearly 20 books from the nursery section of one bookshelf, and then placed them in a stack on an old original oak library desk my dad had restored in his youth.

Satisfied that this would **suffice** for my project, I grabbed two fishing tackle boxes that weren't being used, and headed off for some serious flower picking. As our domestic flower limit for the project was 10, I didn't have to worry about picking anything around the house. And with dinner set for 6 p.m. around our house, my thinking was that my time would be better spent out in the woods surrounding the house.

As I exited the basement, I heard whining and remembered that my Scottish terrier, Scotty, appropriately named after my Scotch like ways in third grade when I managed to get him for free, had been tied to his 50-foot cable **pulley** run all day. Many days, when we were headed off fishing, Scotty would pull me on my skateboard while I pushed off on one foot to keep up a good momentum. So I had to laugh when he just stood there and leaned his head to the side, as if to say, "OK, what's going on? I don't see a fishing pole or a leash." I decided to ignore his attitude problem. I gave him the go-ahead anyway, and we were off in a flash because, as you might know, no dog likes a leash.

As I gathered my **specimens**, I was careful to place each flower in its own separate compartment, and each tackle box handily held 16 individual blooms. After just four trips out, my plywood table was full, just about the time my mom's welcome "Dinner's ready, Eddy!" rang out. As I'd been too preoccupied to do my usual snacking between meals that afternoon, I hurriedly followed my growling belly up the steps to the dining room.

During dinner while our family was gathered around the table I was too busy eating to join in the conversation. This particular night the dialog consisted of my sister and father cracking jokes and doing a good job trying to outdo each other. I casually mentioned that I would probably be up late that night. When the inevitable question arose, I explained the extra-credit challenge and the possibility of an upgraded report card. Since my challenge was school related, my parents raised no objections but reminded me, "No TV, Eddy."

After dinner I walked outside and picked nine flowers from the gardens around our house. Running out of daylight, I cut to the chase and picked blooms out of our homemade flower-boxes, decorated to match the gingerbread trim on our house. Then I walked out past our fish pond, pulled out my Bowie knife and lopped off a single stem of Shakespeare's favorite flower before the darkness settled in. Having filled my **quota**, I embarked on the next phase, which was all desk work.

Fortunately, for whatever reason, I centered my plan on picking only those flowers whose common names were ingrained in my brain and which were indeed the common names. This small point of detail made the task of finding the scientific names mathematically factorable. The two common denominators, so to speak, were the fact that I would have many professional books' glossaries and a common name. This made finding the subsequent scientific names nothing more than a product of these two factors. Find the common name in the glossary and the scientific name would be in the body of the description of the flower. So my mathematical equation was limited only by my time and the amount of product available.

I had been so engrossed in my work that I had paid no attention to the time. But when my eyelids started drooping I looked up at the wall clock and discovered that it was precisely midnight. I stared at my project and wondered, dreamily, if I had won the contest. Not quite convinced, I thought, "Just one more flower, Eddy, and that ought to do it!" The Oregon grape, Mahonia Aquifolium, was my 128th mounting, and my last flower. At 12:30 a.m. I decided to call it quits for the morning.

Fiction in Red II

The next day was a blur of normalcy and **tedium** at school, until it was time for my sixth-period class. One girl, smiling broadly, gingerly laid out her picture-perfect, professionally laminated project—which featured an impressive 127 flowers. Without asking, the teacher just assumed what appeared obvious, and prepared to declare Daisy the obvious winner. That was, until I raised my hand and started waving my arm wildly in objection and protest. In disbelief that my count might actually exceed his now favorite flower girl my teacher had the **audacity** to ask if mine was done neatly. In **defiance**, I carried my project up to the front of the class for John's **perusal**. Fortunately, for Daisy, he was a softy at heart, and he gave us both the extra credit.

For many years, though, I continued to hold the record.

Moral of the story: If it weren't for the last minute, a lot of things would never get done.

5
Motorcycle Madness

W hile I was attending college in Ashland, Oregon, and working, I soon figured out that being promoted to a shift supervisor position wasn't all it was cracked up to be. The tips I had been receiving as a delivery driver far outweighed the $2-an-hour compensation increase I was receiving. Now, I had the added responsibilities of doing the books, scheduling employee hours, locking up, and preparing the dreaded bank deposits. The only real bonus was a deferred one--more experience on my resume.

One warm evening in late July an extremely **scruffy**-looking guy came in and ordered a medium pizza with the works, and a beer. He smelled a little ripe, but he didn't quite fit the homeless-train-hopping-**hobo** profile I saw from time to time in the restaurant. His speech was clear and concise. His hands were clean and his fingernails well trimmed. And he was sporting designer eye-wear and a pair of **Nike Air Max** running shoes.

It was already late and fast closing in on our 1 a.m.

door-locking time, so I let the waitresses go home, and started chatting up my sole **patron**. He was a teacher from California, and for the previous 30 days he had been on the Pacific Crest Trail (PCT)—which runs 2,650 miles from Mexico to the Canadian border. Both of my parents had been schoolteachers, so I naturally proceeded to ask questions about some of the things I suspected they would have had in common. After discussing continuing education, **tenure** and the rock formations near Lake Shasta, I was fairly certain that he was being truthful about who he was and why he needed a break from the trail.

As my last drivers were leaving with their final deliveries of the night, I locked the doors and allowed my new friend, Mat, to share a free pitcher of beer. I quickly finished the closing operations at the greeting station and then joined him at the front table while I waited for my drivers to return. As our conversation progressed, I **elucidated** my own adventures--my day hikes, campouts and cross-country workouts on the PCT between Crater Lake and Ashland. This **piqued** his interest ten-fold, as Crater Lake was where he was to meet his wife and children, as well as his final journey goal. For my part, I was utterly engrossed in stories of his recent exploits on the trail between an area in northern California and the Mount Ashland Ski Resort parking lot.

The **tête-à-tête** that followed was engaging and mutually beneficial. Amusing tales of rocks in the middle of the trail **metamorphosing** into bears and running off, and bighorn sheep becoming nothing more than a misplaced traffic sawhorse on a rocky hillside punctuated our lively early-morning conversation. We even covered the specific details—exact locations of good camping sites and water along the trail—and both agreed that knowing where the permanent horse shelters and potable water can be found is extremely important when one is backpacking.

About 2 a.m., I told Mat that it was quitting time for both of us. After all, I reasoned that he would need to sleep and be up at 8 a m for the Bi-Mart store's opening in order to restock his supplies. I also advised him that he could utilize the nearby Laundromat and be prudently repacked before his 12 noon checkout time at Motel 8 next door.

Mat had agreed with the plan I had proposed earlier: a special outing the next day whose details would emerge later. We met about 10 hours later in the parking lot that conjoined all of the aforementioned businesses.

I had indicated that our daytrip would be an adventure, as my Chevy Cavalier station wagon had lost its second gear. This minor transmission problem had become too much of an embarrassment not to fix any longer. Our alternate vehicle, my KZ 650, had more than enough power to get up the mountain range. But the riders' configuration--I had a **sissy bar** and a touring seat on the bike, and he had a bulky and heavily **laden** backpack—would make us a bit of a spectacle.

When I asked him if he had ever ridden on a motorcycle before, he laughingly admitted that he hadn't. Right then

I knew that we were in for an adventure. I gave him my first-time-passenger rules of the road. I explained that the ground was a whole lot nearer than it is in a car, instructing him to lean with the motorcycle, keep his feet on the pegs and avoid touching the mufflers, which get hot and stay hot. "Most importantly," I said, "You'll have to speak up loudly if you have any questions en route, if you expect me to hear you."

Just getting on the bike was a chore. I had to use the engine stand instead of the kick stand to provide a three-point contact to stabilize the bike. Then I instructed him to mount himself up on the back seat with the sissy bar in-between the backpack and himself. This required my assistance as he was still attached to that backpack! Getting on the bike myself was easy, and with a gentle forward rocking motion we were on our way.

The odd arrangement may have looked like an accident waiting to happen. In actuality, however, it helped to lock him in and kept the normal new-passenger sway to a minimum, which made for a very nice trip to the trail.

The trailhead of the PCT situated between Ashland and Klamath Falls is only a few short miles. The bulk of this journey is uphill on a very curvy road. The road, normally, is not very congested and affords a great view of the valley and a wide variety of trees. The numerous cutback corners winding up and up are a motorcyclist's dream come true. Nothing could have been more perfect, I thought, the sun shining and the breeze gently blowing, than the ride we had up that hill. It seemed that nothing could go wrong--until we stopped.

While we were getting off of the bike at the PCT trailhead, disaster struck! Mat had **ostensibly** failed to heed my advice on keeping his boots off the mufflers. The heels on his $12 dollar discount specials had melted off, producing the **acrid** odor of burning plastic. Not wanting to appear rude before, when the subject of his footwear came up, I chimed in now, suggesting that he could enjoy himself in his **Nike Air Max** running shoes (which I had found, oddly, were a very good substitute for my ultra-lightweight Merrill hiking boots). He scoffed stubbornly, said he would try them later if his feet started to hurt, and we parted ways.

Immediately firing up my bike I had another assignment to tend to. I had to make a trip to a **reservoir** near the Klamath Lakes that had been created to help farmers water their crops. This reserve of water had become a haven for wildlife, for both fish and many types of birds. I was to do a report on a pair of bald eagles that our **ornithology** class had discovered and had been monitoring all term.

This "secret" spot was not far from the road. The eagles were nesting and, to my surprise, now had one **hatchling**. Apparently, the eagles had figured out that humans who carried **binoculars** were no threat, and didn't think twice about people who stopped on the roadside and watched them for hours. Heck, these two stunning creatures didn't appear a bit concerned that I was in a tree less than 20 feet away! I wrote in my observation **journal** about the event, in order to share with the class and help ensure a good grade.

Life went on as usual, with never a dull moment, for about a year, until one day out of the blue I received a letter in the mail from my teacher friend, Mat. He thanked me for the ride and let me know that he had gotten quite a bit of mileage out of sharing his hiking experiences with his pupils. The highlight, which always sparked howls of laughter from the students, was the burning-boot **episode**. He also **acknowledged** that I had been absolutely right about the footwear choice; after coping with a couple of nasty blisters, he put on the Nikes, and then wished that he had worn them the entire trip!

Moral of the story: Listen to the captain of the ship!

6
My Best Day

Stepping out onto the very private deck of my rental house I wondered if I had made the right decision in giving my two weeks' notice at work. I lifted my coffee mug to my lips while enjoying the wooded backyard view of the stream and salal bushes. A slight fluttering in my gut, from either the coffee or the anxiety of not having a job, reminded me that it was too late to turn back. My lease was up, and I had turned over the restaurant keys the day before.

The pull of greener pastures was inevitable in the situation in which I had found myself: working 50 to 60 hours a week, with no time to do much else. That's way too much to give of yourself to any company, unless you are the sole **proprietor**, and that wasn't going to happen where I was. Tipping up my mug to drain the last of the coffee, including the **bitter** grounds mixed with sugar at the bottom, I made peace with the fact that my time in Ashland was up.

Turning to my buddy, Tom, who would drive my fully stuffed Ford Escort to my parents' home, I asked, "Do you want to stop at that bridge near Dillard if it stays this hot?" He smirked from ear to ear, and offered his quick reply, "Only if the bikinis are out, Eddy." I chuckled my way into a cheap grin, and added, "What else do they have to do there when it's 90 degrees out?"

I followed Tom up Interstate 5 from Ashland to our destination. The drive on that chalk-dry day in August was a breeze, as the thought of polka-dot two-piece swimsuits pushed both our **libidos** and gas pedals. My buddy was evidently not aware that he was speeding until I passed him up and forced him to slow down. The downshifting rev of my shiny black Yamaha Virago's 920 cc engine slowed him down just in time before we hit the fully occupied speed trap close to our cutoff. The 90 miles to Dillard was almost exactly the halfway point from home, and we had made very good time.

We parked at the east end of the bridge, changed into our cutoffs behind the car and headed down to the **bustling** water hole. After we laid out our beach towels on the water **sculpted** pepper gray rock we noticed a group of guys taking turns jumping into the water upstream from above the bridge at a cadence of about one every two minutes. Out of curiosity we went over and started up some small talk in order to find out what was going on.

It turned out that these guys were avid fishermen and were taking turns floating down to a shadowy area underneath the bridge. The steelhead were running, and these large two foot long silver-gray fish were congregated in a school of about 100 in the cool shade of the bridge. We took our turn, several times, in order to see these fish in their natural habitat. Seeing these fish eye to eye less than an arm's length away from you while swimming underwater is something everyone should experience at least once in their lifetime.

The natural habitat of the browning blonds also **piqued** our interest, for reasons that are well enough understood by any guy between the ages of 13 and 90. As the river was low this time of year, the best place to sunbathe was on the smooth dark sheets of riverbed which in places had patches of silty smooth black sand. Having laid out our beach towels earlier, before heading up to check out the steelhead, we were pleasantly surprised to discover that a **bevy** of beauties had set up camp right next to us.

As I approached my towel and bent down to untie my soaked sneakers, the faint brush of something nicking the hair on my head landed with a crash. I looked down, startled, to find the label of a Gatorade bottle that had just been jetted by a passenger in a car crossing the bridge— missing my skull by a mere inch. Fortunately, the bottle hit my towel, which kept the glass shards to a minimum and fairly contained.

The scantily clad gal just in front of me was doused with the remaining sticky orange liquid and was sprinkled with some of the larger glass shards. Though prickly sweet, she wasn't bleeding. I also was fortunate in that I was wearing my glacier style prescription sunglasses, and I didn't have any bleeding cuts to my eyes or face.

The **perpetrators**, a group of three locals, were foolish enough to make their way down to the bathing area. The boyfriend of the gal who got sprayed got into a shouting match with one of the guys, who seemed to relish the attention and actually bragged about throwing the bottle. Seemingly, they knew each other and the **scandal-spouting** jerk went unaffected by the verbal harassment.

It was a good thing that my cell phone was handy; amazingly, within minutes of my 9-1-1 call, a very professional state trooper showed up on the scene within minutes. Presumably from his posh speed trap only a half a mile away. Obviously, this riverbed was a hotspot for action.

The trooper gathered all of the information about the incident, and then asked for my driver's license number and phone number. Reacting automatically, I gave him the details, and also my concealed weapons permit number. Semi-alarmed, he bellowed, "You are supposed to tell me if you have a gun." I replied that while I did not have a firearm, my buddy did—and I delivered the information in a tone of voice loud enough for the hooligan to hear. Smiling at the slightly smirking officer, I asked, "Why do you need my information, officer?"

"Since no one was injured badly enough to go to the hospital, I can only give him a $1,000 dollar citation for littering," the officer replied, while obviously trying not to laugh. "But," he added in a loud voice, eyeing the now very nervous-looking young man, "since he's a local, if he tries to fight it in court I can charge him with attempted manslaughter--and lock him up with your eyewitness testimony."

Leaving our cozy paradise, I turned to Tom and asked,, "Why, when we are together, do these types of things always seem to occur?" Shrugging and ejecting the shell in the chamber out of his Luger 9 mm, he replied, grinning, "Just lucky I guess."

Minutes later, we were ready to get back on the road toward home.

Taking the lead, my buddy edged onto the two-lane road in my little white car. This narrow winding road followed the river from Interstate 5 to our coastal homes. Following at a safe distance on my motorcycle, I saw an oncoming car swerve suddenly to the left, followed a split second later by my white Ford Escort veering sharply to the right and then back to the center of the road. I automatically downshifted to third gear and decelerated to 45 miles per hour, trying to size up the situation.

Seeing a four-point buck scrambling to get up off the pavement was the last thing I wanted to see. He was up on his front feet, so I knew that I had to drop to second gear to try to decrease my speed and keep some power to try to keep control. Goosing the throttle, before the impact probably saved my life. I had never had the front wheel of that bike off the ground, even though I had tried many times. But somehow it came up this time and landed onto the back of that unlucky deer.

Coming down on top of a deer is something you don't want to do at 45 miles an hour pulling a wheelie. Fortunately, the screaming engine took the brunt of the forceful impact, killing the buck instantly. The jarring force of my bike coming down on the pavement bent both of my front forks, and the next five seconds was a fight for my life.

Instead of flipping over, the bike had become lodged on top of the unfortunate deer. Somehow the buck had gotten entangled and wedged under my bike. It was pinched, or rather pinned, between the rear wheel and the substantial engine stand mechanism. I was now hunched, chin into the speedometer, while braking with all of my might and using all of my skill trying to stay up.

For the next 50 yards I fought the jittering handlebars and the mêlée of my unwanted passenger. Coming to an uncontrolled, but nonetheless upright stop just feet from the embankment leading to the river, I shuddered in relief. I hit the engine's kill switch on my handlebars and looked down, shaking. The buck was dead. When I raised my head, Tom was driving backwards toward me, screaming out the window, "Eddy! Are you OK? Did you miss him?"

"No, Tom, I killed him," I replied gravely. Laughing, he said, "No, you didn't. Where is he?" Pointing down below me, Tom was now as shocked to see the lifeless carcass as I was. The gruesome scene was now before us. The last 50 feet of my ordeal was plainly marked by a three-foot-wide swath of blood and hair ripped from the deer's hide.

Looking at me in amazement, Tom issued a nervous chuckle, and said, "Man, you are the luckiest person I have ever known. There are people who die when they hit a deer while in their cars, and you just walked away from hitting one on your cycle! I can't believe this you have escaped death twice in the last hour."

Smiling at Tom, I crossed my still shaking arms across my chest to stop them from shaking. Walking it off before I finally calmed down, I looked over to my buddy and said jokingly, "Maybe we should stop and buy a lottery ticket when we get home."

"Then I want half!" Tom laughed.

Moral of the story: If you're having a bad hair day, try counting your blessings.

7
My Worst Day

If you were to go back in time and remember your favorite field trip in school, which would it be? Most people have their favorite **reminiscences** in that realm, but the question becomes: Would you relive it?

Every now and then, when I see one of those perfect, one-in-a-thousand smiles, my memory steams backward to my Susan story. I met her while I was on one of my **extracurricular** English class field trips, during my sophomore year of college, while taking advantage of an inexpensive package to see a couple of Shakespearean plays in Ashland.

When we arrived in our school's mini bus, the eight of us found that there was a **hierarchy** involved in the accommodations. Our professors stayed in a **posh** bed and breakfast, while the students were **relegated** to the economical youth **hostel** down the street.

The arrangement suited us all well, until I met Susan, who was working at the hostel for the summer. For an incredibly beautiful and well-educated woman, she was an **anomaly** of sorts in that she was a nature-loving, outdoorsy type. She enjoyed hiking, skiing and camping, and she was a runner to boot. Unfortunately, she also had a job down at the health food co-op, so we didn't get to visit as much as I would have liked that weekend. As I was leaving, I asked if she would like to take in a play two weeks later. She **nonchalantly** said, "Sure," and added, "as long as you are staying here, we'll figure something out."

Since Susan had a day job I reasoned I might as well get in a couple of good days of skiing on my upcoming visit as well. In fact, skiing was almost as important as getting to know Susan better. Thus, besides my regular college studies, the next two weeks were relegated to planning a combination ski trip, date and theater excursion.

My first order of business was to organize my ski equipment, which took an entire day. The second day I spent poring over the play schedules and reading up on the story lines of the plays we might see. The next 10 days went by like an unwound clock.

Finally, the Friday in February of the much-anticipated date came, and my front-wheel-drive station wagon was loaded and good to go. Or so I thought. Just about 100 miles into my journey to the Ashland Youth Hostel I sensed a slow unraveling beneath the vehicle. In seconds I realized that the "thump, thump, thump" sound I was hearing was the tread on my "new" studded retread front right tire coming right off.

Fiction in Red II

Slowing down I found a safe place to pull over and inspected the damage. From the looks of the tires I realized that both front tires would have to be replaced. Since I only had one spare tire, I determined that it would be a waste of time to change just one. Getting back on the Freeway I stayed at 40 miles per hour with my hazard flashers on. Fortunately, it was only a matter of a few short miles to the first exit.

I pulled off Interstate 5 at that exit and found a gas station that just happened to sell tires. Unfortunately, it wasn't a Les Schwab dealership franchise (where I'd purchased the originals), so I had to pay through the nose to replace them with two brand-new unstudded tires. Another 60 miles up the road, predictably, the back ones came unglued. Fortunately, the Les Schwab dealership in Medford did guarantee the rear tires, but the shop didn't have any studded tires in my car's size.

Arriving at 8 p.m. at the Ashland hostel wasn't something you wanted to do if you had any intention of staying the night. At 6 o'clock sharp there was usually a good crowd at the door waiting for it to open. First come, first served is the rule for hostels, and backpackers always take precedence. Fortunately, it is usually slow in winter and getting a bed was no problem.

Inquiring of the on-duty hostel host I found out that Susan had the night off and was out on a date. We hadn't confirmed anything, so it all was OK as far as I was concerned. The wait time also freed me up to fill up my gas tank and do some studying for school. When she walked in with a guy, obviously returning from her date, it didn't bother me too much. After all, Susan and I didn't really didn't know each other very well.

After the date left, I told Susan why I'd gotten to town late, and asked her if the guy would have a problem with us seeing a play together the next day. "Oh, no, Eddy," she assured me. "He's just a friend."

After reviewing the play guide, we made arrangements to see a Shakespearean comedy at the Black Swan Theater, a venue well known for its intimate performances. The opening curtain call would be at 7:45 p.m., which would give me time to go skiing. The late call would also allow her to go to work and also fulfill her hostel duties, from 5 to 7 p.m.

When I took off early the following morning, the weather was stormy. The snow was coming down in steady heavy flakes and sticking to the ground like pepper on mashed potatoes. Stopping briefly at Bi-Mart store to try to purchase some chains I found that it didn't open until 8 a.m. Brushing off the chains' purchase as an unnecessary expense, I wasn't concerned. I had made the trip up to mount Ashland many times before without the aid of chains or studded snow tires.

Entering Interstate 5 off of Siskiyou Boulevard I charged up the snow-packed pass easily enough for the first two miles. Then, when I rounded the first big bend of Siskiyou Pass, I witnessed total **mayhem**—about 50 cars angled in various positions, their drivers clearly not in control of the situation, were blocking my path. This snarled pile-up had been caused by a sheet of ice, which had blocked off all of I-5. The officer in charge stood there barking orders at us. "No one can pass this point without chains period—and that means no one," he said. Since Bi-Mart was just down the road, I literally pushed my car to the side of the road sideways on the ice and started walking back.

I arrived just as the store opened, which was a relief, as many of us have learned the hard way about how aggressive tow-truck drivers can be when they come across apparently abandoned vehicles. I decided to buy two expensive high-traction sets of chains, a no-brainer after having slid my car off to the side of the road by hand—one hand, that is. Within two hours of my morning start time I had made my way to the Mount Ashland ski lodge. I found the parking lot nearly empty, as most of the people in front of me had to be towed. I would have little competition conquering the hill, I thought happily.

Jokingly, I asked the cashier if there was a discount in place for nasty days. "No," the nasty man replied, without a shred of humor. "If you want to go skiing, it's still full price today." I contemplated the factors of wind and wet snow, and took into account the fact that I had exactly enough money in my wallet for a one-day ticket. It seemed like a good **omen** for me to buy the ticket.

Eddy Ivy

I walked back to my car and placed my wallet in my gear bag, thinking that I wouldn't need it again until I hit the ATM machine later than day. Switching my snow boots with my ski boots, I trudged through the mushy snow to the ski lift.

With only a dozen cars in the parking lot, the skiing proved terrific from the standpoint of the crowd factor. The weather, on the other hand, was so bad that after four hours I was the only one still skiing. When it finally started to rain, I decided to call it quits. When I walked up to the parking lot, my car was nowhere to be seen. In fact there were only three cars remaining in the entire lot. In disbelief, I hurried to the front desk and told them of my problem. Since there were no phones working on account of the storm, I caught a ride with one of the ski patrol staff members. Unfortunately, he lived on the California side of the mountain, so the best he could do was to drop me off at the I-5 exit.

Walking in ski boots is no fun under the best of conditions, but it's a real drag when you have no money and no car, and you're 200 miles from home in the middle of a snowstorm. The situation was **exacerbated** by the fact that I-5 had been closed to all northbound traffic all day long, giving me no prospect for hitching a ride the last 10 miles to Ashland.

A few miles into my hike I saw a rest area on my right. The "urge to go" was the least of my worries, I suppose, but I was getting a little uncomfortable, so I welcomed the chance to rest and pull myself together. Walking out the restroom door, a pleasant surprise greeted me in the form of a car—which was like a mirage to me after the two hours I had just spent trekking the freeway shoulder. The pass had just opened, which meant I would be able to hitch a ride. Watching the man get out in a suit and tie to take off his chains gave me an idea. "Sir, I'll take off your chains for $3," I offered excitedly. Handing me a $5 bill, he laughed wearily and said, "It's a deal, kid. Keep the change. I'll be back after I use the head."

Looking at my watch and realizing that I had six hours before my date started, I moved into machine mode. I set up shop right there, and within an hour I was stuffing my pockets with cash—and charging whatever I figured the cars' occupants would pay.

Time became a blur. Since the rat through the boa constrictor lasted for four hours, the only thing on my mind was money, money, money. My parents and sister were away on vacation, and as my wallet was in my car, the sudden income stream was a godsend. Although the night was falling and flow of traffic was **ebbing**, I decided to hold out for just one more "customer."

A little red Porsche pulled up. The driver was a middle-aged gentleman, who was wearing a gold chain and a bright floral Hawaiian shirt. I presented my now-standard (for established-looking types) line: "I'll take off your chains for $5 dollars, sir."

Smiling, he said, "You've got a deal. Take off those chains!" He walked off toward the restroom, as I started the process of undoing his tire chains. When he returned, he eyed me quizzically, and said, "I can't help but notice that you've got ski boots on, young man. What's up?" When I told him what had happened, he reached into his wallet and pulled out a $100 bill. "You probably don't need this, but heck, you deserve it," he said.

Thanking him **profusely**, I decided that I was in no position to argue. Waving at him while he left, I realized that he had been the only person to notice, much less ask about my dilemma. After servicing a few more cars and telling myself again, "OK, just one more, Eddy, then you're out of here."

It wasn't long before a midnight blue Firebird drove up. The driver, a gorgeous brunette was wearing a stunning red form fitting **angora** sweater. "How about $3 to take off your chains, Miss?" I asked, in my most pleasant business tone. Her reply was a complete surprise. "Now that's not very gentlemanly like of you," she said, giving me a hard stare.

"I know it isn't. I'm sorry," I said. "But someone stole my car and everything I had for my trip which was in it and I'm just trying to get together enough money to make it home. See my ski boots?" The retort was swift and stinging. "Serves you right!" she said. Even though her remark was unforgivably rude and condescending, it struck me deep. Looking around at the empty parking and then directly into her eyes, I said, "You know, lady, you are very lucky that I am indeed a gentleman."

Turning and walking to the men's room I walked into a stall, and, despite the smelly surroundings, took a breather. I really didn't want to go out until she was gone. For the lack of anything else better to do I decided to tally my earnings. It was an unbelievable $386! At that point, I made the decision to "go home."

Two minutes after I stuck out my thumb, a man in a green Chevy Suburban stopped and picked me up. "Where would you like me to drop you off, son?" he asked jovially. "Well, the police station would be nice," I said, in a mildly joking tone. When he asked why, I recounted my story—for the fifth time that day. He dropped me off at the Ashland Police Department and handed me a $20. "Good luck, kid," he said. I stood there slightly astounded at the range of human response I had encountered in the previous hour, and just had to smile. Thanking him and commending myself for having the good sense not to tell him how much money I had made—who knew, after all, that the guy would be a straight shooter?--I closed the door.

I tromped into the station, and all eyes turned toward me and my noisy footwear. I spoke to the officer who came to the counter, and told her about my plight. Expecting to be asked to fill out forms, or at least to have her call and put out my car's license plate number on the radio, I was shocked by her nonchalance. "I can't find the right forms," she said.

"Come back tomorrow morning." Still in disbelief, I asked her to tell me the quickest route to the youth hostel. She drew a rough diagram, and said, "Take this road up to Siskiyou Boulevard. I pointed down at my boots, and said, "At this point, I need the shortest route; do you have a map?"

She reluctantly offered more detail, saying that the dirt road behind the station would lead straight to the hostel. "But you really need to take Siskiyou" she ordered in what to my mind was a nasty tone. In reality the decision to take the shortest route had already been made by my now aching feet.

Trudging through the seven inches of snow for about a mile was no fun. Even with a little more than $400 in my pocket, my head was slumped down the whole way, as I pondered what I was going to do the next day. Then, without warning, I walked smack into the back of a car. Startled, I looked up, in shock. I had walked into my own car, less than 100 yards from the youth hostel. It was locked. Unbelievably, nothing had been taken.

I searched high and low, but found no evidence that any lock had been forced or that the ignition had been hotwired. Either someone had a master key or my car had been towed. Since I always record my mileage, gas price and miles per gallon in my homemade register I checked the odometer against my booklet and deduced that the vehicle had indeed been towed. The odometer had clocked only 24 miles since I filled the tank the night before. That distance would have been the approximate mileage up to Mount Ashland. Who took my car and why bugged me intensely. The other perplexing fact was that my car had been abandoned less than 100 yards away from the hostel where I was staying.

Since the hostel's parking lot was surrounded by a laurel hedge, I felt comfortable that someone wouldn't try to steal my car again. Parking in the last available spot I locked the doors and proceeded to walk inside. As I stepped into the living room I sensed something wrong. A police officer with a notepad was talking to the man who owned the hostel. Just then a young woman pointed me out to the officer, and said, "Hey, he's the guy who was supposed to take Susan out!" Walking up to me, the officer asked me if this was the truth.

Not knowing what was going on, I blurted out, "Yes, I was supposed to meet her here." It turned out that Susan had missed her shift that afternoon, and I was the prime suspect in her disappearance. While I was breathlessly **recounting** the day's adventures, it dawned on me that the officer's attitude was changing. Because my story was so incredible, despite being true, I started to have a gut feeling that I was getting myself into trouble, the longer I talked. At about the time I began the part where I had walked smack dab into my car, Susan and another one of her "friends" walked in. She had totally forgotten about her shift at the hostel, and had gone out to dinner on a **whim**.

Looking at me sternly, the officer said, "You are lucky that she walked in, Eddy, because I was getting ready to detain you just because of all the lies you were telling me." I asked him to accompany me outside for a private conversation, and he agreed. I produced a huge wad of bills, and said, "Sir, this has been the worst day of my life." Looking back at me, he gave me a knowing glance and said, "Well, Eddy, if I were you I wouldn't waste my time with that gal." Then he walked back to his car shaking his head.

It was too late to make the play, so Susan and I decided to go see a movie instead. *Das Boot,* I think it was.

Moral of the story: Resources are all around you, but it is up to you to fully utilize them.

8

Old Snaggletooth

My year working at Mount Rainier National Park was **harrowingly** close to its end, and I was reluctant to leave until I had accomplished all of my objectives. One of the things on my summer to-do list was to go to the opposite, eastern side of the park and visit Sunrise. It's a nice little tourist trap in its own right, and it offers a different perspective of the mountains grandeur with respect to that of the historic lodge at Paradise.

Sunrise is situated high on the mountain and is a favorite starting point of mountain climbers who are looking for relatively less risk in climbing to the 14,408-foot summit. The "town," is also the highest point that a visitor to this dormant volcanic peak can drive up to. Besides featuring the regular tourist **amenities**, it had a big draw for me: free food for park employees!

When I arrived at the food catering area, the menu was somewhat limited compared to what we were used to at Paradise. My selection--a ham sandwich, a Coke and a bag of

Doritos--was tasty, but not quite enough to fill me up. Since I was still a growing boy in a man's body, I always made sure that my car was always stocked with extra goodies, so the meager meal wasn't going to present a **predicament** later.

My normal hiking buddy was filling in for someone who was sick, so the outing was a lone adventure. I made my way to a vacant picnic table, extracted the bountiful morsel from the small brown bag and laid it out. After taking a few bites of the sandwich, I walked over to a **knoll** a few yards away and took some prize-winning shots with my Canon camera of the eastern side of the mount.

Turning around and walking to my table, I came face to face with Bullwinkle--a bit of a shock, to say the least. My rational realization that the beast knew he was protected provided me some relief; I figured he likely was somewhat docile. Given where I was, sighting a 1,200-pound bull elk wasn't a particularly surprising event. Seeing that thieving **herbivore** dive in to my ham sandwich, however, was.

Walking towards Bullwinkle, I cautiously snatched my Coke just as a female ranger came up and shooed him off. "You're not supposed to feed the animals," she barked loudly, shooting me an unwarranted look of disgust. My reply was as swift and as disrespectful as hers, matching her tone and her shrillness on the decibel scale. "At $8.50 a sandwich, do you really think I would give him my meal? He stole it, I tell you, so why don't you go out and arrest him!" I exclaimed, glaring back at her.

Fiction in Red II

Frustrated and startled by my blunt comeback and steadfast gaze, she huffed sternly, did a 180-degree about face, marched through the dirt fast enough to kick up some dust, and then sped off in her cruiser. I had no choice but to go back to the canteen to buy another sandwich. After telling my tale of woe to the manager, he produced a complimentary meal, which was bloody well civilized of him, I thought. He told me that the meal-stealing elk was named Snaggletooth because he had a chip in his left front **incisor** and would eat anything, including a world-famous Paradise ham sandwich!

Going back to the same table, I encountered Snaggletooth once again, who was then munching on leftover chips that the ranger had accidentally swooshed off the table while trying to get rid of him. This time I managed to hang on to most of my meal, but Snaggletooth made away with a few carrot sticks and a Baby Ruth bar. The reason he got the candy bar was, frankly, that he had about 1,035 pounds on me. Spying his prize, he **gingerly** nudged me with his snout and literally knocked me off the picnic table backwards, as if to say, "Thanks, sucker!"

Back at Paradise Lodge I gave an account of my run-in with a **carnivorous** elk. My story was met with obvious disbelief, with the exception of a couple of rangers who told me that they were glad to know that Old Snaggletooth was still alive. It seemed to be that he was a well-known figure among the park's senior rangers. It turned out he had been mooching off tourists for many years. "Just like Yogi Bear in Jelly Stone National Park," quipped one ranger, "but no one really knew how old he was."

A few weeks later the season ended, and I vowed that I would make an annual **pilgrimage** to Mount Rainier every summer. The second year I was accompanied by an old girlfriend from college, Carmen. In keeping with the Eddy Ivy tradition, the campsite of choice was classified as "primitive" by park officials. In fact, it happens to be the nearest "official" campsite south of Paradise Lodge.

The drive to the campsite from Portland had taken an unusually long five hours due to a flat tire. My personal policy is to have a flat tire repaired at the first opportunity, which in turn had almost doubled the normal three-hour driving time. Exhausted, we just set up camp and went to sleep. In the morning, I woke to a shuffling sound. Peeking out the mesh netting window, I spotted a dozen elk bedded down about 30 feet away. Waking up Carmen with a kiss, I said, "shhh" while pointing out in their direction. She looked out as the mighty family of elk ambled upright. Peering over her shoulder, I spied what I thought might be Old Snaggletooth. I wondered if it could be possible that he was over here on the west side of the mountain away from the crowds and free handouts.

Remembering that we had fruit in a **rucksack** I pulled out an apple, a banana, and two granola fruit bars, and unzipped the tent door, just as the elk were starting to wander off. At this point, with nothing to lose, I bellowed "Snaggletooth!"

Fiction in Red II

To Carmen's astonishment, and my own, frankly, about 30 seconds later the mighty beast emerged from the brush and started ambling towards me--a little too fast for my comfort zone, since I did have a girl to protect. At the last second, when his hoof was just a yard from my foot, he stopped, leaned toward me and ate the shiny red apple right out of my hand.

Then he helped himself to another apple, both bananas and then the granola bars. When he had wiped out our stash, I raised my hands, fanned them, and said, "Shoo, go away." Taking my cue, Snaggletooth turned away, walked a few steps and stopped. Then he shot me a backward glance and then trotted quickly down a well-worn trail to find his friends.

Looking at me with her hands on her hips and consternation in her eyes, Carmen said, "OK, Dr. Doolittle, what are we going to eat for breakfast?"

Moral of the story: Don't feed the animals!

9

Pinnacle Peak

S unday brunch in Paradise Lodge on Washington's Mount Rainier is only one of many good reasons to work in a national park during the summer months. As it turned out, 1993 was an especially good year for that culinary experience because we had a retired **merchant marine** head chef in the kitchen. **Rumor** had it that he had spent time on one of those huge oil rigs down in the Gulf of Mexico, and the men on those rigs just won't tolerate bad food, if you know what I mean, translated into our good fortune.

My good friend, Tom, and I were waiters at the main lodge. Due to the weekly buffet-style **banquet** on Sunday we didn't have to wait breakfast, a break from routine that we really appreciated.

We took advantage of this **respite** from work and took short hikes, under five miles in length, and were generally able to get back in time for lunch. That was a far better meal than any other served during the week, **reputedly** and also in our humble opinion. In memory, some of the more **zealous** crew would entertain the guests by dressing up in Austrian garb and chanting a silly song that went something along these lines:

"Hi, ho, hi, ho. It's off to brunch we go. We've starved all day to get this way. Hi, ho, hi, ho, hi, ho, sing it again."

You get the picture. But let me **reiterate**: It was very good food.

In order to be back in time, to be the first in line for the 11 a.m. brunch, we had to leave by at least 4 a.m. for an average hike. One of our most memorable hikes in early July was up to the top of Pinnacle Peak. Not only is it one of the most **prominent** landmarks at 6,562 feet as seen from the observatory below the main lodge, but it has an extremely well groomed 1.3-mile trail to its **saddle** between it and Plummer Peak on the Tatoosh range. Starting in darkness and arriving at the Reflection Lakes parking lot, we joked that no one—aside from us, that is–was crazy enough to be out so early and that, as usual, we would be the first to reach the peak.

We started at the trailhead at an **altitude** of 4,860 feet, and we didn't encounter a single soul except for a rather large marmot who was a little boisterous and probably hoping for a handout. This of course he did not get, not because we didn't want to feed the little fellow but because all of the room in our small mountain backpacks was occupied by every bit of camera equipment that we could fit in them.

You see, this hike is well known for its great photo opportunities. It sports great views of pristine meadows, the Nisqually Glacier, Mount Adams, Mount Saint Helens, and Mount Hood, not to mention the best view of Mount Rainier you will ever see in your life.

At about one mile into our hike we were caught off guard by another cute but annoying little rodent, the Pika if you're from Washington, or Coney if you're from Oregon. All the rest of the known universe calls them rock rabbits, from what I've been told. Their bark is worse than their bite, if you ever encounter one of these critters. They live in rock fields and have a habit of sounding out a shrill *"eeeek"* warning always at a point just about when you feel completely relaxed. This little shock gave us both a good reason to stop and catch our breath, as we each always tried to outdo the other on these short but punishing hikes.

Arriving at the saddle, the wonderfully kept trail ended abruptly, as well as the darkness. The view of the distant peaks in front of the morning sun was stunning--and it was another great excuse to stop and take a swig of Gatorade from our bota bags. Assessing our topo map we decided that the last leg of our journey was about 420 feet, nearly straight uphill. We also deduced that the average person wouldn't attempt the 40-degree incline to the top.

Slowly, we moved single file up the face, carefully sashaying between the anchored rocks and boulders, being careful not to step on the **fray** of the loose rocks and dirt.

We were both experienced free climbers, and we had been **chiding** and chuckling at each other most of the way up as we had both slipped up ever so slightly already. Reminding each other that we were in a dangerous position, we started using a technique known as a three-point stance. This is accomplished by keeping a hold on the mountain using three points of your body in constant contact while you **ascend**, which reduces your chances of falling.

Fifteen minutes into our climb we were closing in on the top when, to our astonishment, we were **pummeled** by what seemed to be a mini landslide! Looking up, we saw the silhouettes of two men already on their way down. The realization that we weren't the first to reach the top that morning wasn't the biggest shock, however. We were absolutely dumb-founded to discover that one of the climbers was 73 years old, and that his partner, **brandishing** a cane, was a tender 91!

We couldn't help but ask, a bit breathlessly and out of intense interest: What time did you have to leave to beat us up here? The wisecrack from the older of the two caught us off guard when he replied **cynically**, "At our age you don't get much sleep anyway," "so 2 a.m. isn't really that early for us," chimed in the younger of the two.

Laughing at him, Tom politely asked what they were doing on the mountain, at this time of day and under these notoriously difficult climbing circumstances. After all, it had to have been still dark when those **intrepid** seniors were climbing to the top. The younger man blithely replied that his companion was, in fact, his father, and that the two had hiked together their entire lives. "We're very used to the routine. When I asked the father if he was afraid of getting hurt, they **sagely** replied in unison, with a chuckle, 'At our age, son, it really doesn't matter, now does it?' !"

Moral of the story: Beware of the man who has nothing to lose!

10
Pizza Blitz

My delivery-carryout Pizza Shack in Medford, Oregon, was the cleanest, most **sanitary** restaurant in the United States—or at least in my not so humble opinion of how I had achieved this end. Being a bit of an organizational neat freak, I was a little concerned about the cleanliness of my restaurant. I also knew that the health inspectors always come around at the worst possible time just to see how you are doing. Not to mention the fact I didn't want anyone getting sick from the food at my restaurant, including myself, which upped the ante.

After some hard thought I instituted a rule that my manager, the owner, and area supervisor all applauded: No employees could go home until they had cleaned their assigned zone to spotless perfection. But within a couple of weeks of implementing this rule, I began to notice some rumbling and countering influences within the ranks.

As I was working mainly with high school students, this "clean-zone" rule had other interesting effects. Those workers who only wanted to man the phones and take on no other duties now wanted to go home earlier, due to this twist in the law of reverse psychology. The ability to **wean** the blood-sucking lazy bums and keep on the real workers really helped to keep my allotted personnel-hours time goals in check. The allotted personnel-hours finally jumped out of the red and into the black.

It didn't take long for the franchise owner to notice how much cleaner my restaurant was than his 10 other eateries. Taking an interest in my innovation, he presented me with a challenge. All of the carry-out Pizza Shacks across the country are **vying** for the title of who can pay themselves off the fastest. It wasn't an order but rather an implied, "show me how good you really are" offer. Unfortunately, at that point all of the other Pizza Shacks had a seven- to 13-week head start on me.

I **surmised** that because I was only the assistant manager, I could achieve my objective only if the owner, Mr. Bigshot, was willing to fire his lazy son-in-law boy Robin, who was going to college full time. Boy Robin came in for just a couple of hours a week, and when there was more of a **hindrance** than a help. At least that salary reduction would have given me a reasonable chance of winning.

Regardless of my lack of interest of lining the owner's ego, I did run a tight operation--and I humored Mr. Bigshot from time to time. I had turned our slugs-on-salt-blocks delivery drivers into Indy car champs by utilizing the new computerized printout comments section to create precise directional maps, thereby cutting delivery times in half.

One of my more notorious cash-cow endeavors was engaging in what you might call anticipatory suggestive pizza "pre-sales." Here's how it worked. I knew that the Sunday pigskin event of the year, the Psycho Bowl, was going to be a nightmare for all of the pizza joints in town. So I decided to act **preemptively**, in a sense, by having my phone operators call our regular customers and guarantee on-time delivery if they would pre-order their pizza at least a week ahead of time. The hundreds of phone calls my staff made in the two weeks before this cherished annual event netted a modest return: Twenty-two customers actually pre-ordered their pizza. What I suspected, however, was that I'd planted a seed.

When the owner walked in a week before the big game and asked what I was doing to prepare for the big crush, I told him that I had put everyone in the store on the schedule and added, "But I could use another 20 workers." He laughed and said, "Eddy, I'm sure that won't be necessary."

When I reminded Mr. Bigshot that I had an MBA in marketing and was planning on selling at least twice the number of pizzas any of his other greasy spoons would ship out, he said, "Are you serious?"

"Well, yes Mr. Bigshot, I am," I confirmed. "Can you spare anybody from your other stores?"

"What makes you so sure you'll need more staff?" he asked. "Well, I was counting on having people pre-order—and we've got some of those orders on the books," I said. "But I think it will turn out that I have succeeded primarily in reminding customers of where to call first." Advertising over the phone in this manner has proved highly successful in other business **venues**, and I projected that my failure to fully succeed in the initial pre-marketing effort would turn the place into a free-for-all the following Sunday. And at that point, there would be nothing anyone could do to adequately manage the order volume which would surely follow.

Neither Mr. Bigshot nor Boy Blunder was buying it. They didn't heed my warnings, and no reinforcements were brought in, which meant that only 22 customers got their pizzas on time. By the first quarter the four phones were red hot and the girls who were usually calm, collected, prim and proper were sweating from the heat of the pace for once. I was actually enjoying myself at this point, and couldn't resist laughing to myself.

My nice, sanitary restaurant had become carpeted in cheese and pepperoni. It was a good thing that the health department didn't come that week, as we were in a major clean-up mode for the next two days. My only consolation was that I was exactly on the money regarding the number of sales I had forecast and pizza dough I had ordered to be made up in the morning--which was all of the pans in the store. I must say it was awfully satisfying to see Mr. Bigshot running out, his brow drenched in sweat, to deliver pizzas!

Finally, nine months after the competition for national bragging rights for the first concept store to be paid off started, our big day came. My store was paid off about one week after the first one, in Chico, California, broke even. "Well, Eddy, you failed," was all that Mr. Bigshot could say, even as he mentally patted his wallet.

I, on the other hand, already had other plans. I had worked with and gotten to know the national franchise vice president's daughter years before, at another national Pizza Shack chain store, and had kept in loose contact with her. When I called her up out of the blue one day and told her what had happened, the right authorities were promptly informed of this minor injustice. In fact, as my Pizza Shack had paid itself off in the shortest amount of time, we were the true winner of the trophy-less contest.

Within weeks, all of the Pizza Shack **dignitaries** were **traipsing** into to my pad to see what made it so special. To their amazement, we had managed to create the poster child of all Pizza Shack stores--even my hot thermal delivery bags were clean and shiny! I dispensed loads of advice, answered too many questions, and kept the root beer running freely. And once I had established myself as the king of Pizzadom, I walked up to the owner and, without one **iota** of reluctance, gave him my two weeks' notice.

Moral of the story: Give credit where credit is due.

11
Red Stag Camp

Anyone who has ever been employed by one of those big companies that uses a rotating schedule and forces workers into odd days off knows just how frustrating it can be to structure one's social life. Landing a job in the freight industry I found out that Big Brown was open 24-7. As a new hire for this **behemoth**, I was also informed that my weekends were to be Sunday and Monday, on the worst shift they had.

After about two weeks on my new job I was getting acclimated to my new schedule and was fully ready for a weekend getaway. While getting ready to head off for a camping trip, the thought of facing a full campground in the middle of Oregon really hadn't crossed my mind. In addition to the tent, bag and food the prospect of a relaxing weekend fishing was the only thing swimming around in the back of my mind.

Lining up the special trailer my father had constructed specifically for my camouflaged vessel, I lowered my canoe onto it and used a couple of motorcycle cinch straps to secure it firmly. I grabbed my anchor of a tackle box and attached a red shirt sleeve to the end of my canoe to serve as a safety flag—then the weekend officially started with the click of a master padlock, which secured my trailer to my truck.

I arrived at Timothy Lake to find it crushingly overcrowded, which prompted me to realize that it was Labor Day weekend--another thing that hadn't registered. The campsites were overflowing, the overflow parking was past capacity, and it was still early morning on Sunday. I decided that since I'd gone to this much trouble, I might as well do a little fishing anyway, so I went out a little past the casting limits of the folks who were fishing on shore.

When it occurred to me that I wasn't catching anything, and might not for awhile, I decided to get some exercise by rowing my small craft to a corner across the lake well away from the crowds. A few minutes later an Oregon Fish and Game officer came up and asked for my license. Being used to this inconvenience, I handed it over. He briefly glanced at it, then handed it back and then proceeded on his way across the lake to precisely the spot where I was headed.

About 10 minutes later the sight of two young teenage boys on air mattresses made me **wince**. Looking and seeing that they weren't wearing life preservers, I asked what I thought was the obvious question, **bluntly**. "Hey, do you need a ride?" They responded with an **adamant** "No," even after I pointed out that they were way too far off shore for safety. They became more **belligerent**, so I proposed a challenge. "I bet you're both too tired to pull yourselves up into my canoe without using your air mattresses," I said, in a more friendly tone than they deserved.

No real boy would refuse that challenge, was my thinking. But as it turned out, neither could pull himself out of the lake. My point, then, had been well made. With the help of their air mattresses they were able to **hoist** their frames into the boat and we headed off to the designated swimming area.

Having a captive audience in my vessel, it was difficult to resist the urge to **reprimand** them by sharing a few stories of the mistakes I had made when I was younger. My reasoning and the lessons I **imparted** went over better than I expected; and by the time we had reached the boat dock, there was no need for parental discipline. They both thanked me, sheepishly, which was evidence that they then knew how **Lilliputian** their foresight had been.

Heading back toward my previous destination, I wondered why the deputy who had demanded my license hadn't even slowed down for the kids. Was the revenue from fines and fishing licenses really more important than the welfare of our youth, I wondered? Mentally shaking my head and unhooking my frustration I focused on my next task. Finding my secret **moorage buoy** was my key to comfort. It was located in a shady channel at the northeast neck of the lake.

Fiction in Red II

Years earlier, when I was in my teens I had sunk a Styrofoam salt-water buoy 10 feet below the surface in precisely this spot. It was attached to a 100-pound rock and I could attach my line to it fairly easily because there was a loop of rope on the top. Casting out in the shade, I resumed fishing. It took awhile, nearly a six pack of Pepsi, but I finally caught a fish. It was a small rainbow trout. A couple more like that, I thought, and my dinner would be well supplemented. That turned out to be more laborious than I expected, but **Powerbait** on a treble hook attached a few feet down from a red-and-white bobber can work wonders if you give it some time.

I started to head home and it occurred to me that home was more than two hours away, not a particularly exciting proposition after a long hot day of paddling a canoe. Making an executive decision between me and myself, I decided to follow one of the many old logging roads that led away from the lake towards Highway 26. There I would set up camp in a spot decently removed from the end-of-summer, last-ditch party scene for which Oregonians are so well known. I headed north from the campground and minutes later discovered a single-lane gravel road off to the left of the pavement, which proved too tempting to pass by. After about a mile I **deduced** that the road was not well traveled.

Even without my 20-foot trailer and canoe, there were no turn-outs generous enough to enable me to physically turn around a vehicle. The sides of the road were flanked by large ditches on each side to **divert** water during the heavy rains of winter and spring. It was sort of like traveling down the Great Wall of China. The only comforting thing was that, looking down at my dashboard, I realized that my gas tank was almost full. One mile turned to three and then to five, before I finally spotted a pull-out.

Carefully backing into the sparsely used area using my **peripheral** vision I stopped short of the stream. Checking my other mirror I was startled to see a painted **rendition** of a red 6-point buck on the side of a towering Douglas fir. When I had turned off my engine and hopped out of the cab, the display of a **deer hang** that hunters use after a successful hunt caught my eye. And just across a small stream, I spotted what to my sore eyes looked like the **idyllic** camping spot- -flat, punctuated by two large fire rings, and with plenty of left-over firewood onsite. To boot, I was miles from anyone, as far as I could tell.

Thinking that my discovery was too good to be true, but unloading my tent and trusty Coleman lanterns anyway, I pursued my task of setting up camp with **unabashed** joy. I started a fire and cut off three green alder saplings, then proceeded to fashion my trout into a rough skewer—my "fish on a stick" routine. After counterbalancing the boughs with a few extra rocks from the stream, the fish met their final fate while I cracked open a home-brewed root beer.

The fish were tasty, the weather warm but not terribly hot, and the forest was so dense around the camp that the imminent sunset couldn't be seen. In what seemed just a mere two minutes, my camp was pitch black. For awhile, the firelight produced a sufficient glow--enough to enable me to clean up all of the dinner implements. But soon, I couldn't proceed without lighting my lanterns. Throwing all of my uneaten food into the fire to discourage critters from visiting, and locking my cooler of food in the cab of my truck, I pulled out a rare copy of **Rudyard Kipling's** Illustrated "Boy Stories."

It was a copy that my grandmother had given me when I was a boy, by mistake, I now think. The stories were better suited to being read by high school graduates who were soon to start college. Perhaps the gift was to broaden my vocabulary, but I doubt that my silver-haired grandma would knowingly give me such a coarse book to read. The **graphic** nature of this collection of English adventures in India, were a bit too much for me to comprehend when I first encountered them in sixth grade.

At 12 years of age, I wasn't ready to grasp the **nuances** of the decidedly British vocabulary or possess sufficient knowledge of English history to fully enjoy the book. Now at 29 years of age and some change, I opened the book to my favorite story starting on page 371. The Strange Ride of Morrowbie Jukes is a great story about eating crow that everyone should read at least once in their lifetime. After about an hour, the lanterns began to dim. It was time to call it a night.

I poured just enough water on the fire to extinguish it, and pulled another brimming bucket from the nearby stream and set it next to the door of my tent. Per my usual mode, I let both of my lanterns go out naturally. That is to say that I normally don't close the off valve, which in turn allows the gas pressure to decrease gradually. This creates a pleasant dimming light and makes for a nice transition into dreamland.

Turning on my **halogen** scuba light hanging from the top of my old blue tent, I found the process of getting comfortable easy. I was all alone, however, so I loaded up my 9-mm stainless steel P85 MK II semi-automatic handgun. Chambering an extra hollow point slug and putting a couple of extra clips under my pillow, I turned off my light and quickly fell into a sound asleep.

At about 3 a.m. I sensed an eerie presence of light outside, which roused me from my deep sleep. At first, I thought it merely a light from a passing vehicle on the road, so I closed my eyes and waited for it to pass some 50 yards away. But I didn't hear any accompanying sound, which prompted me into a full state of alertness. The whites of my eyes could have lit my tent in that moment of shock. Now was a time think quickly.

The light in the area was gaining, slowly brightening my campsite via the interior of my tent. Trying to calm myself, I nonetheless realized that the forest canopy and brush were simply too dense to allow light through. So I moved into action mode, slowly pulling my gun out from my sleeping bag and quietly clicking off the safety.

Fiction in Red II

The light was getting stronger, and as it intensified, I began to distinguish blue and red hues. This told me that the moon likely wasn't the culprit, as I knew that the **rods** and **cones** in human eyes can't readily distinguish colors at night. The last bit of evidence that my now very alert mind processed was that the angle of the light was shining horizontally, at a roughly 10-percent angle.

I knew that game wardens generally don't work at night, so I went on the offensive, calling out, in a loud, gruff voice, "Identify yourself now!" In a split second I also made the decision to place my finger on the trigger.

Bang, Bang, Bang, Bang, Bang, Bang, Bang, Bang, Bang, Bang, Bang, Bang, Bang, Bang, Bang, Bang! I shot through Old Blue, knowing that anything that might have been alive on the other side of the tent was now dead.

Dropping the clip and installing another, I quickly chambered another round and sliced an opening on the back side of my tent. Scrambling out the back, I crawled on the ground **infantry style** to the far side of a large tree. Peering into the blackness, I saw the culprit exposed. A fine moonbeam was moving through the forest, it elegantly cut through my camp like a white laser beam. In all of my 25 years of camping, I had never seen so fine a ray as this. It only lasted a mere 15 minutes, which was just long enough to rid my body of the huge excess of **adrenaline** pumping through my veins.

Eddy Ivy

I crawled back inside what was left of my tent, basking in the comprehension of what had just taken place, and my heart stilled, then warmed. Old Blue had been a good and faithful servant for 20 years and was way past retirement. This trip had fulfilled another chapter in my life and ultimately propelled Old Blue to his final destiny—making him holy.

Moral of the story: If you shoot the moon, make sure it's worth it.

12
Sandski Bums

My buddy, Tod, had access to an old Dodge Power-wagon with a **winch** that could have pulled in the moon if we had a cable that long. Tod's father, Bob, had given him free rein of it; the only stipulation was that we had to bring him two cords of wood for the winter before summer was over. Within a week of starting our high school sophomore summer vacation Bob had several cords, split, stacked and delivered.

Our first project after paying it off so to speak was to paint the old workhorse. Since sandy brown was the special of the week, we did as professional a job as one can do with a makeshift plastic covering. It was so good we named it Paint. Next, we picked up some old fat, oversized tires, which don't dig into the sand as much as thin tires do. This trick along with letting out some air pressure comes in handy if you are plucking logs off of the beach.

For the next two years Tod's Dodge's primary purpose was hauling wood. I, too, had an old GMC truck; I had named it

Canvas because of the tarp I used to cover my loads. It wasn't a 4-wheel drive, like the Dodge, and therefore couldn't make it out to the beach. This was important because we could get prime fir virtually anytime we wanted by going out to the Oregon Coast's Horsefall Beach, and didn't have to pay for wood-cutting permits either.

The plan was simple: leave my truck at the main paved parking lot and go out in the Power-wagon and slice up logs into easily moveable rounds. This would take about two hours or less to get a full load. As the two trucks were almost the same height, we would lower the back bed gates. Then we would put my empty truck back to back with his full truck.

This transfer worked picture perfectly, as we easily hand rolled each round evenly from Paint to Canvas. Then of course we would repeat the sequence.

Whether we were cutting firewood on the beach in a 4x4 or gathering logs at a permit site, it was clear that our parents knew well the value of these unsightly beasts of burden and the effort it took to keep them in operation. My parents also knew (and convinced me) that going out to **salvage** yards and taking off parts to your heart's content can build character and more importantly save money. Even though these two junkers were just that, we both took a certain amount of pride in the vehicles. That was exhibited in how fervently we undertook the vehicles' constant upkeep and how artfully we kept the trucks running.

Fiction in Red II

As I was only 16, the effort and expense required to keep the two pickups in sound mechanical shape was quite the financial eye opener. I had to master the fine art of not only spotting good parts but also wrenching them off in a matter of minutes, a skill set that gave me a healthy respect for money. The first time we saved 80 percent on a used part that would normally have cost us 50 dollars, a day's wages cutting wood at that time, I knew I'd contracted junkyard fever, and a **penchant** for saving money also.

Besides accomplishing a lot of work with the pickups, we found time to put the vehicles to other uses as well. They came in handy, for instance, when we needed to haul around three-wheelers or tow an ailing vehicle; and they proved invaluable on hunting trips and, sometimes served handily as basic, if not particularly attractive, transportation. In short, we utilized them well.

My favorite expedition in the Dodge was once when we headed out to Horsefall Beach to attempt something new and exciting: waterskiing on the sand behind a truck. One hot summer day, we packed up a **mahogany** water-ski that Tod had **fabricated** in our high school wood shop class—another one of the myriad of crazy projects we dreamed up that the shop teacher said would never come to **fruition**—and drove to the beach.

As the day's outing evolved, we soon discovered that Tod's **concave** ski performed marginally better in turning on the sand than that of his original flat-bottomed board. For that reason, we weren't afraid to stretch our limits on trying to carve back and forth behind the truck. This, we discovered the hard way, was fairly abrasive to both the board and the rider after a while.

Basically, by using a ski rope tied high on Paint's tailgate, we were able to ski in the soft sand. Unfortunately, we had been unsuccessful in figuring out how to carve as if we were on water without crashing. On finally arriving at Ten-mile Creek, after we'd each endured several spectacular wipeouts, we sat down to ponder whether the **merits** of sand-skiing were worth the effort and how we might adjust both our style and our expectations of our crazy dream.

During that brief brainstorming session, we came up with an exciting idea: We would try to ski from the soft dry sand into the water up the stream for about a half-mile and then back on to the sand. Looking at one another wide-eyed, it appeared that we had abandoned the notion of addressing the initial problem and instead let it simmer on our minds' **backburners** while we tried our new venture.

Since Tod was the better water-skier he tried the first run from the beach into the stream. After three wipeouts in a row we agreed that we needed a new course of action. We turned off the engine, looked out over the **curvature of the earth**, and started discussing why the ski took off like greased lightning when hitting the water.

We deduced that when the ski was free from the friction of the sand, the only way to counteract the loss of control was to attempt a hard cutting turn outward into the middle of the stream. In order to successfully pull this off, we decided to use a longer rope. This change would enable us to make a long curving **arc** whereby the skier could lean out hard into the water at the instant of the ski moved from sand to water. Tod was the first to figure out how hard to edge to make the perfect transitions. From there on out, it worked like a charm!

The new problem, we then **hypothesized**, was to figure out how to go from the water to the sand. I agreed to go next and function as the guinea pig for the second part of our hare-brained scheme, and within minutes I had experienced a spectacular crash that we would later describe to friends as "the wipeout of the decade."

Starting in the water was just like waterskiing, only behind a truck. Traveling at about 25 miles per hour upstream I crashed and burned when I hit the sandy edge of the stream. It was like landing on a sheet of sandpaper as hard as concrete. This crash took most of the outer layer of skin off of half of my body. While relating the exhilarating experience of becoming Mister Hyde-less I related with Jeckel-less **exuberance** on how badly I needed another "gentler" break.

After we positioned the truck out toward the ocean and contemplated the waves, we turned our attention to the only exciting activity of the moment: watching Tod's two black Labradors frolicking in the surf. It was a good thing that they weren't in the cab with us, as the dogs probably would have been licking our wounds with their salt-watered tongues.

Throwing around new ideas for smoothing out our surf-to-sand ride wasn't working too well, until we witnessed Tasha, the hyperactive pooch of the two pulling in an extremely large branch very slowly from the water.

"Hey!" I exclaimed. "What if we slow down just before we exit? Since the stream is flowing down and the ski tip is curved up, we should be able to keep our balance." Even at two or three miles an hour, I reasoned, we would be able to gauge the resistance needed to stay up. Then we could ski as long as we wanted.

The solution worked well, even if our new "**circuit**" was kind of choppy. We got in a few decent rides, to the apparent amazement of a small group of onlookers who had parked their dune buggies to watch the free show. Unfortunately, the tide was coming in fast, so we soon headed home bruised and battered, but still buoyant from our long day of fun.

Moral of the story: There is a good reason why it's said that dogs are a boy's best friend.

13
Sea Dogs

E arly one morning, at 6:45, I opened the door to my favorite coffee shop, the Beanery. Bright and early every Saturday I would visit this veritable land of eternal sunshine. In fact if I wasn't there by 7 a.m. I would get a coffee call from a lonely Barista, my girlfriend Sunshine, who only worked there on Saturday's.

Normally at 6:45 the haunt would be bustling, but not on the weekend. This solitude gave us time to chat and plan our schedules for the upcoming term. While drinking my second small mocha I was almost ready to give up on my Southern Oregon State University schedule. Nothing looked interesting until, by chance, I came across the category "advanced" Scuba Diving classes, 1 credit. Since I had previously completed my Open Water 1 and 2 certifications, among others, I turned to Sunshine and asked her what she thought about it.

Unexpectedly she whipped out a Professional Association of Divers card (PADI) and said go for it, but this is the only card I will ever need for diving. While meeting with my two professors that afternoon, I asked what they would want me to do to obtain a cave-diving certification. It turned out that I would have to teach the Open Water 1 class every Friday, and lecture on various subjects like night diving and high-altitude diving. I would also be in charge of setting up special projects, such as simulated night dives and obstacle courses. This was of course in addition to my Cave diving course work.

After two months of classes, which were held five days a week every morning at 7 am I felt I was ready for my cave-diving certification test. This, of course, had to be done in a cave in the ocean. The certification was to take place about 900 miles away from Ashland, off the California coast near Catalina Island.

Fortunately, for me this trip shaped up nicely in comparison to many of my other adventures. Sunshine wanted to visit her parents, who lived in Los Angeles, which took care of finding a place to stay. Gas money was provided by my two instructors who were flying down and paid me 100 bucks to **tote** their gear in my Chevy Cavalier station wagon. Rich, my now long time dive buddy decided he wanted to go on the trip also and **anted** up some money to share the back seat with the scuba gear.

This made the trip a lot more enjoyable for me. Originally I had planned on subsisting on dry oatmeal and 32-ounce Big Gulps. With the advent of Sunshine, Rich and the extra cash, we could afford the five-for-a-dollar day-old burgers that the gas station mini markets sold to starving college students like us. Man, those were the driest burgers I have ever loved, all the way to LA, I might add.

Saying good-bye to Sunshine late the next morning, Rich and I were off to Dodger Stadium. I had been persuaded by Sunshine's father, Jimmy and Rich, again, to take in another Dodgers baseball game live. Despite the fact I didn't catch a misdirected foul ball in the stands, the Dodgers won as usual and we both had a great time.

We arrived at the **marina** where our dive boat was moored with about a half hour to spare. Everyone else had already been there for hours, hanging around and basically engaging in tourist-type activities. After loading our gear on board I had the good fortune to begin a conversation with the very **amiable** first mate of our chartered dive boat. I asked him what the limits on lobster were, and he said, quite hurriedly, "If you want lobster, you had better hurry up the street and get a license. We leave in 20 minutes." I literally ran up the road to get the license. Fortunately, they had an out-of-state three-day permit that was very reasonable.

The first day out and about the island, the trip went very well; Rich and I both got a couple of really good dives in. We saw a variety of sea life, including moray eels, a stingray, a multitude of fish and dozens of seals. Unfortunately, our mesh goody bags were empty, as we hadn't so much as even seen a lobster. This was probably a good thing, given that Rich hadn't purchased a license!

Eddy Ivy

That evening, while everyone else was enjoying the warm California breeze, I was at the **helm** with John, the dive boat's captain and owner. I mentioned that I hadn't had any luck finding any lobster. He asked if I had a license, and I readily produced it, enclosed in its own zip-lock sandwich baggy. He then turned to my college professor, who had just wandered in, and asked if I was night-dive qualified; my instructor verified that I was with a quick nod. John then asked me if I was willing to do a night dive. I was stunned at his matter-of-fact attitude about something that was, to me, a very big deal. But the opportunity to bag lobster and get in a real night-diving experience in the ocean instead of a pool was just too good to pass up.

Despite the fact I was tired from the long trip down Interstate 5 two days before and my two dives that day, I eagerly grabbed by Diver's Log Book. Looking at the chronicled entries of my duration in the water, and the depth I had gone down to, I determined that it wouldn't be safe for me to dive until 3 a.m., according to the Navy dive tables used by NAUI. Turning to the captain, I asked in a quizzing but upbeat tone, "Is 3 too late?"

John looked at me, laughingly but pleased, and said, "Sounds great, Eddy. Get some sleep, and I'll have the first mate come get you at 3 a.m." At 2:30 a.m., the first mate shook me, and I was up in a flash. Looking at my Casio alarm watch and then back at him, he didn't give me a chance to ask why he woke me up early. "Dude," he said, "you've got to get ready--and my shift starts at 2:30, not 3:00." I was too pumped up to feel any tiredness and whispered back to him so as not to wake my bunk mate, "Dude, I thought I had overslept!"

John and I met on the **aft port** side of the boat, and he promptly taped one red glow stick to each my two air-supply lines, near each mouthpiece. I hadn't seen this maneuver before, but in pitch darkness, it's a safety move that makes good sense. He also produced 10 green glow sticks, attached with electrician's tape to used tire weights. When I asked what they were for, John said, "Well, Eddy, they're going to mark the tunnel out of the cave." I looked at one of my instructors, who was the dive master that night. He said, "Oh, by the way, I talked with your instructor and you are getting your cave certification tonight. That is, if you pass, he added **forebodingly.**

I blurted out, "Cool, but could you at least clue me in to what our dive plan is?" John provided the details. We would swim the quarter mile to shore on our backs to **conserve** air. Then we would double-check our gauges, air pressure and dive accessories, and then go over the dive's specifics, just before we descended to the cave entrance. He added, "Remember, Eddy, this is for your cave dive certification, and we need to know how you will deal under pressure."

At the cliff, we stopped. John rattled off the specifics:

"We are going to descend to about 60 feet and swim along the bottom until we reach a **V-8** engine block. We will then ascend to 40 feet, where there should be a four-foot-wide tunnel about 60 feet in length. I will go in first, and you will follow about one minute later, when you hear me blow this whistle. When you make your way through the tunnel, swim 50 more feet and ascend to the top of the cave, where I will be waiting for you at sea level."

At the entrance I did as I was told. When I heard the whistle, I proceeded through. I noticed that John had placed a green glow stick every 10 feet of the tunnel floor, which had the desired effect, I noted, of indicating where the bottom was, as well as where the various trapped air pockets from the previous divers had been caught. It occurred to me that this set-up might prove extremely useful in an emergency situation.

Suddenly, I was startled by something forcibly pulling my air supply from my mouth. **Instinctively**, I grabbed for my **second-stage octopus** spare air on my buoyancy compensator. Upon further inspection, I discovered that it was a **crag** on the top of the tunnel that had caught my **primary** air supply. After correcting this little **mishap**, I continued down the corridor. On exiting the tunnel, I noted that my depth gauge read 39 feet and that John had left four glow sticks in a semi-circle. I also noted that fact, and then proceeded up to where John was floating upright in the middle of the cave.

John said, "Good job, Eddy. You're now halfway home on your way to cave certification." Then he upped the ante. "Here is your test. This cave is about 200 feet or so in diameter and we are now at sea level, as evidenced by the fresh air you are breathing." (I reasoned that there must be another exit, or at least an air outlet through the cracks, and that made me feel a little bit more secure.) "Furthermore," John stated, "there are hundreds, possibly thousands of lobsters below us, but as soon as we go down, there will be a mud cloud from the **silt**. Visibility will become almost nothing. Your test is to wait here for 15 minutes, then go down to ground level, fill your bag with as many bugs (lobster) as you can, and try to find your way back to the boat. That is the test; if you are not out of the cave in 45 minutes, I will come back and meet you here."

As I repeated the instructions back to him, I added, "I assume that I should keep blowing the whistle as I go through the tunnel on my way out?" He nodded, and said, "Good, see you soon."

The first five minutes of waiting wasn't too bad as John's bright white scuba light lit the huge cave well. After ten minutes however, an Othello like transition took place. Soon the cave had become black from the silt. John had been gathering lobster left and right, and stirring up so much muck that I was wondering if I would even be able to find any of the prized **crustaceans**. At 15 minutes, I descended to the bottom and found that he was correct: There were hundreds of lobsters for the taking.

Filling my bag was easy. It took me less than ten minutes to grab about 40 lobster, which handily filled my almost gunny-sack-sized goody bag. At that point, I realized that I had to get out. I stopped and thought to myself, OK, I know the depth of the exit is 39 feet, but which way do I go? Then I remembered an old secret to getting out of a tall maze, just start walking along any wall and keep the wall on the right. You will eventually find your way out, I reminded myself, to calm my racing heart.

I went up to 40 feet, and started swimming in a straight line. I found the wall in about 197 seconds. Then I did the same trick as one does in a maze; but I was swimming instead of walking.

After about 300 feet, I happily found the four glow sticks, but I was presented another problem. The sack of lobsters couldn't be pulled or pushed because they would catch on the tunnel's crags. I stopped, and thought to myself, OK, I need to get this bag **neutrally buoyant**—but how? I checked the pockets of my **buoyancy compensator**, and found my small white mesh goody bag, which contained a bread sack with two stainless steel safety pins and four zip-lock sandwich baggies. It occurred to me that I could fill up the baggies, put them in the bread sack, and then position them in the small goody bag and attach it to the end of the big goody bag full of lobster. My air supply was down to 1500 pounds down from 3000, so I still had plenty of air, I reasoned. Then caution set in. "This had better work Eddy, or you're going to be in serious trouble," I mumbled mentally to myself.

Bingo! It did work, and to make it still easier to **maneuver**, I put the buoyant air bags inside with the lobster, which made everything more compact. Into the tunnel I went, picking up the entire line of glow sticks one by one as I moved along.

Upon exiting I found John. He gave me the thumbs-up, and for a split second I thought he was saying "good job." Then I remembered that the thumbs-up signal meant go to the surface! So I gave him the thumbs-up, and we surfaced together. He grinned from ear to ear and said, "Eddy, in the last eight years of taking people to this secret cave nobody has ever made it out. And by the way, you have 10 times your limit at least!"

I laughed nervously, and said, "Well, you told me to fill my bag, and besides, look at yours. You have about 20 lobsters!"

He chuckled, eyed me sagely, and said, "The hardest part is going to be getting back. We have a lot of big **undulating** waves coming at us in our way. What you suggest we do, Eddy?" I looked at my gauge, and said, "Well, I think that we should burn as much air as we can underwater at about 10 feet, while heading east towards the boat. Then, when we are away from the shore and waves, and out of air, our tanks will help buoy us up."

John looked at me in amazement, and said, "As soon as we get to the boat, you're officially cave certified, young man!"

Descending to 10 feet, I was in for a surprise. A **litter** of seal pups started hounding us mercilessly. John kept on going, doggedly. But I was **perturbed**, to say the least. I stopped and turned, and fended them off, as they were no match for my secret weapon.

Back at the boat, John and I were basically all alone except for the lone dive master, who eagerly hoisted up our catch, and then logged our entry back on board.

After **donning** our swimsuits, standard **attire** for the boat, John once again commended me in front of my instructor, saying that I was the first student to get out of that cave by himself. He was doubly impressed, he added, at how I had gotten my huge catch out. Then he asked me, "I just have to know, Eddy, how you **curtailed** the wild dog's pursuits." I told him the story about my friend, Brent, who had once cut up a glow stick, and how it had filled the water of his fish pond with thousands of **eerie** glowing-star like bubbles. While I had never done it before, I had realized that I had 10 fully loaded glow sticks to play with—and a mission to accomplish. I further added, "When an idea hits me, I just naturally go with my **instincts**."

John smiled, shook his head, and emitted one of those **guttural** chuckles that you can only accomplish by keeping your mouth closed and exhaling through your nose. Then he fixed up a big pot of salt water in the galley, as he got ready to honor our new guests for breakfast.

Moral of the story: When presented with a problem, stop, keep your cool, and use your head.

14
Snow Wonder

Have you ever thought to yourself, I wonder what would happen if … and then done it? Back in the summer of 1982, when I was just starting college I had the opportunity to take the path less traveled. That, in and of itself, is normally no big deal, but the **conundrum** in which I found myself after taking what had appeared to be a substantial shortcut now makes me think twice before venturing out of bounds.

On my way to Mt. Hood, the charming hamlet of Welches boasted a well-posted forest information station, which **beckoned** me in as I drove past. I walked in and asked the blonde desk ranger if there were any **primitive** campsites located near an established trail that also featured a good view of the mountain. Without batting an eye, she handed me a double-folded flyer and replied, "You're in luck. The Mirror Lake trail fits the bill and it's now the most popular trail in Oregon."

When I ventured, playfully and with a blazing smile,

to ask which trail used to be the state's most popular, she jumped right on it. "The Oregon Trail, silly," she said, popping her bubble gum and laughing. "And if you want to see the original ruts of the wagon trail you need to stop about a quarter mile before you get to the Mirror Lake parking area," she continued matter-of-factly.

Laughing at myself, I replied, "Guess I stepped right in to that one. By the way, is there any way to easily spot the trailhead so that I don't go too far?" She confidently instructed me to "look for about 20 cars on the side of the road in the middle of nowhere, or keep your eyes open for a bright red bridge hewn out of a log." With a seductive grin she then held up her left hand, which still had smidges of red paint from her endeavors painting the foot bridge, and a small but elegant sparkler on her ring finger.

"If you get to Ski Bowl—it's got a huge sign bragging that it is the largest night ski area in the United States-- you've gone a half mile too far," she said, in a decidedly professorial tone that was at odds with her perky personality.

Blondes should stay in California, I muttered to myself as I started back for my car. Out of love and any measurable luck, the swooning of desire had subsided the second I had seen her promise ring. Re-focused on my journey I reached for my oversized soft drink on the hood of my car, and finished it off in a manner befitting the "Big Gulp" name printed on the cup. A few miles up the road I caught sight of the red footbridge. Parking in the fifth unmarked space from the stream's crossing, I unloaded my gear and pulled the distributor's main wire slightly to disable my car and deter theft, as I figured I would be out for a couple of days.

I was locking the hatch of my station wagon when an attractive brunette drove up. I asked her where she was headed, and she said, cockily, "To the top, of course." After a little small talk about our respective objectives, we were off. Her name was Kathleen, and she had taken the day off work to get in some hiking. Mirror Lake trail was her favorite hike, she divulged, and she had come to take photos to inspire her paintings.

I told her that I wasn't camera shy, and she quickly pulled out her camera and started clicking--joking that she wanted to see if her boyfriend would get jealous. After a few minutes we stopped and signed in at the trail register. I asked if the entire trail would be as easily traversed as the previous quarter mile. Kathleen warned me that there were two markedly different components of the hike to the summit. The first was the mile-and-a-half trail that zigzagged steeply up to the lake; the second was a seemingly vertical 1.5-mile climb that followed the outside of the **crescent** cliff that encircled the lake. Fortunately, I was in great shape from running, and my 40-pound pack wasn't holding me back.

When we arrived at the camp area near the lake, my decision to refrain from committing to a campsite became easier when I realized that the only amenity was an outhouse. I decided to plow ahead with my full pack and enjoy her company, while managing the equivalent of a very good workout from carrying the extra weight on my back. When we reached the top Kathleen she wasted no time in shooting a couple of rolls of film.

We shared a lunchtime meal and I remarked that the intense heat was propelling me towards a swim. And the lake, beautiful and clear on this cloudless August day, beckoned. "In fact," I pronounced, "I think I'm just going to hop off this ledge and jump from tree to tree into the lake from here." She laughed in a tone suggesting disbelief, and said, "Go ahead. I'll take the trail back, if you don't mind."

"So, Kathleen, will you join me in a swim?" I asked. She agreed, and I started making my way down the steep cliff-like embankment. "What are you doing, Eddy?" She asked. "That's too dangerous!"

"Well, if I am correct, this shortcut will save me at least 30 minutes off of my hike to the lake--and remember that I still have to set up camp, I explained. "So, are we still on for the swim?" When she offered a confirming nod, I was off.

The first 75 yards of my path consisted of rocks and boulders, which made it fairly easy to hop from one to the next on my way down. I thought to myself, just another 300 yards and I'll be at the lake. I had spoken, if silently, a bit too soon. Seven yards later I was up to my eyeballs in Avalanche Trees. From a short distance these trees look just like shrubbery, but any experienced mountain climber knows that if you ever find yourself in their midst you are trapped like a fly in a spider's web.

What had happened was that the weight of snow had bent these alders in the shape of crescents. Their four-inch trunks were protruding from the embankment horizontally instead of vertically, and then curved upright to their normal erect position. In addition to this abnormality, the branches had been forced from the weight of seasonal snowpack to grow out from side to side instead of symmetrically; creating an irregular jumble that had ensnared me.

Suddenly, I had one of those truly sinking feelings. But vanity intervened momentarily, when I muttered to myself, "I really hope Kathleen isn't watching this spectacle!" I had been struggling for at least 10 minutes, and I clearly wasn't making any measurable headway. Looking up to the top of the hill, I scanned the ledge, and was relieved to discover that no one could see my **predicament**. That's **ironic**, I thought, I'm pinned like a rat in a trap, and I don't want anyone to know I'm in danger!

The harder I tried to proceed through the field of branches, the deeper into trouble I got. Now, 20 feet into a span of shrubs may not seem like a big deal, but in reality I would have been in trouble even without the additional weight of my backpack. I was stuck on a 45-degree slope; it was time to stop and think. Since my **vantage** point included the strange formation of the trees' trunks horizontal at my eye level, I pushed down on one and came up with a plan. If I could somehow hoist myself up on this bouncy bough and hang onto the side branches of the accompanying trees, I could pull myself slowly up and out of this trap.

My first attempts were **futile**, as I tried to crawl up in the middle of the curved crescent in front of me. The springy nature of the bend of the tree mimicked the actions a hobby horse would make. Stopping again and thinking, I surmised that the closer I was to the base of the trunk, the more stable and rigid my platform would be. The strategy worked. I was able to take three steps directly on top of the **stock** and then step up to the middle of the next tree up the hill.

Out of the snare, I turned around and laughed at myself in one of those moments of inspiration to which we're seldom **privy.** Why not just reverse the process, I thought, and walk down the middle of one tree to the next one. Cautiously traversing the middle of the first tree four or five steps, I found that my weight would press the tree to bend downward nearly three feet. Then, by launching my weight onto one foot, I could spring up as if on a diving board and easily step to the next tree with my other.

Using this technique, I managed to bounce my way down the entire length of my poorly chosen shortcut. In just a few minutes, I was clear of the avalanche trees and had arrived at the base of the lake. Despite my 10-minute delay, my **flailing meanderings** had saved me almost half an hour. Of course, I have to admit that the prospect of seeing Kathleen in a wet T-shirt may have played some part in my persistence!

Fiction in Red II

Setting up camp was a breeze, as on many previous camping adventures, my best-laid plans hadn't worked out— and I ended up hiking well in to the night before making camp. The experience of being forced to set up my tent in darkness due to rain on several occasions; I had devised an easy way to identify each individual support pole. This I accomplished by using two different sets of poles of the same length but of varying girth. By feeling the size and shape of the **couplings** on the ends, I could set up my tent, nicknamed Old Blue, in 10 minutes, even in total darkness.

Now, as it was two in the afternoon and I was in full charge of my **faculties**, I set up Old Blue in a mere five minutes. Unrolling my self-inflating mattress and sleeping bag, the urge to relax for a few minutes overwhelmed me. I closed my eyes and must have drifted off, as the next thing I remembered was Kathleen nudging me with a gentle kick, and saying, "Hey, you still owe me that swim!"

"Gee, what took you so long?" I sputtered nervously, laughing but also praying that she hadn't seen the **folly** of my ways. "Oh, I found another roll of film and stopped to shoot the western valley on the way down," she replied.

I looked at my wrist watch and discovered that it had been more than an hour since we'd parted on the trail. "Would you like to use my tent to change?" I asked nonchalantly.

She gladly borrowed one of my T-shirts and changed into it in my tent. She emerged modestly. "Do you think anyone will know the difference between these and a swimsuit," she asked? Seductively she lifted up my shirt to reveal her red **satin** panties with a smile. "Fooled me," I said, grinning and trying not to stare too hard. Laughing, she dropped the shirt and dove into the lake.

The swim was fun and, of course, way too short for my liking. I could have stayed with her in the shallows all day at that point. Emerging from the clear blue water we shared my only towel and dried off. Ever trying to be the gentleman, I escorted her the 1.5 miles to our cars. Seeing her off, I felt a little lonely and oddly **bereft**, despite our brief acquaintance.

"Oh, well. That's life," I thought, chuckling as I looked at my watch and considered that I still had time to get a good three-mile run and do the avalanche trees one more time before the sun would set!

Moral of the story: Sometimes the solution to your problem is right under your nose.

15
That New-Car Smell

From the age of 14, I had always owned a street-legal vehicle of some **capacity**. Whether it was a Honda Hobbit moped for basic transportation, an ancient GMC pickup truck for cutting and selling firewood, a Volkswagen dune buggy kit car for fun; or my self-customized four-cylinder Chevy van for ski adventures, I always possessed multiple **modes** of transportation. Fortunately or unfortunately, as the case may be, I paid cash for each vehicle. My parents didn't care what I owned or drove, as long as I paid for the vehicles out of my own pocket.

On my 17th birthday my parents began impressing upon me the importance of establishing a good credit history. To underscore their point, they even offered to **co-sign** on a loan for a new car, if I wanted one.

Money really wasn't a problem, even then. From the time I was in third grade onward, I always placed half of my earnings from odd jobs in to a savings account, (on which my parents had, of course, been co-signers). My enterprising nature and willingness to do just about anything to earn a buck gave me the foundation I needed to realize what the magic of compound interest was all about.

I had shoveled snow, mowed lawns, and raked leaves. I sold bottles, aluminum and copper for scrap. I picked ferns. I traded "commodities" (baseball cards and comic books); worked in the school cafeteria, and I even baby-sat--which enabled me to amass a little more than $10,000 by the age of 17. (Fortunately for me, none of the girls I went to high school with knew about my small fortune.)

One day, for the heck of it, I went out browsing for wheels, and found a year-old Honda CRX, which got an impressive 50 miles per gallon. I tried to bargain down on the price and terms. The young salesman eyed me incredulously, and said; "Look, you're not old enough to buy a car this new, even if we lower the price. I don't want to waste my time, and I wouldn't even bother the finance manager with your request."

I wanted that car badly enough that I took my dad down to the dealership that evening, only to find that the car had been sold by another salesman a few hours earlier. Not only did that salesman lose a sale, but when I told my classmate, whose father owned the dealership, what had happened, that salesman was soon looking for a new job.

On the basis of that experience--or failure, as I saw it--I began to understand the importance of a good credit rating.

It really didn't matter what I drove into a dealership or how much money I had in the bank. The fact of the matter was this: At that point in time, I couldn't sign my name for anything, even with my parents' generous offer to co-sign on a loan.

To drown my sorrows, I decided to go out and look at as many cars as I could stand to test drive, and after about a month, I came across a screaming deal. The car was a Chevy Cavalier station wagon with 22,000 miles—making it nearly new, in my opinion. Even better, the car was barely a year old and it was priced $2,500 under the low end of the Kelley Blue Book range.

The salesman attributed the rock-bottom price to the car's high mileage, and then **divulged** that a fishing tackle salesman, whose territory covered Oregon, Washington and Northern California, had been the previous owner. I somehow couldn't believe that, and kept prodding the man for more information. He smiled, quickly looked to the left and then to the right, and then offered in a hushed tone, "The real reason it's so cheap is that it's a four-cylinder, and it has no get up and go. It's come back on to the lot twice, as folks don't like that inconvenience."

Undeterred, I said to the salesman, "Let's take it for a spin. I'm a lot more concerned with gas mileage than pick-up speed, and I've got a KZ 650 that will do 50 in first gear if I want." He laughed, grabbed the keys, and a minute later I found out firsthand that the Cavalier didn't have any get up and go. That didn't matter to me either, as my van had a four-cylinder with a three-on-the-tree manual shift, on a half-ton frame--and its pick-up speed rivaled that of a slug on a salt block. To make a long story short, I called the parental units, went to the bank, got a loan against my savings, bought the car, and drove it home that evening.

That weekend was to go by as weekends usually did: too fast. My buddy, Tod, and I had entered one of those 10 K Pepsi Challenge cross-country races in Lincoln City, midway up the Oregon coast. We packed up our wetsuits, sleeping bags, surfboards, camp stove, food, and the rest of our usual excursion provisions. Our goal wasn't to win the race, or even to test our **mettle** by surfing in the extremely cold Pacific Ocean. It was nothing that normal. Rather, we were in it for the cool T-shirts, which we "collected" at each event and tourist trap where the races were held. Oh, yeah, and did I mention the gals in their skimpy running attire?

On the way back home the surf was flat, so we had plenty of extra time to stop at a not-so-secret but **virtually** inaccessible beach off an infamous part of coastal Highway 101. The only way to get to it was to either take a boat or use technical mountain climbing ropes and gear to descend the 160-foot **precipice**. We had done this climb several times before, so it was pretty much a mechanical process. **Rappelling** down was easy, and gathering the exceptionally large black mussels to barbeque was like a break of sorts, in comparison to the climb back up.

Fiction in Red II

Having learned from past experiences, we didn't tote cumbersome buckets down the sea cliff. Instead, we saved time and frustration by using thick plastic bags to haul up our catch which also meant we had to develop a fun way to get them down to the secluded beach. So that they would survive our 100-foot-plus freefall toss, we put the bags in a couple of nearly **indestructible** Army backpacks, and then added a rock or two to improve their **ballistic trajectory** to the beach. Upon our beach landing, we quickly filled the bags to our legal limit, and we were ready for our arduous climb back up the cliff.

We had already foreseen a good catch, and so had filled a five-gallon bucket half full of saltwater earlier that morning. The night before, we stayed near the Devil's Churn State Park, a rugged, scenic place I always stopped to enjoy even when I was not camping. The park is a pencil-like fissure in the volcanic rock where the Pacific's waves drive through and create a pulverizing crash. The resultant force forms a swelling rush of water, which races up toward a small cascading waterfall on a steep sheer-cliff embankment. The resulting gravitational backwash then recedes and violently clashes with yet another wave and churns the water to a white creamy consistency. It is there in the lull between the surges that one easily pulls out a good bucket of fresh salt water.

Thanks to the marvel of watertight snap-on lids, we were able to dump our precious **cargo** into what was to become their self-cleaning journey. One time-honored trick for cleaning out shellfish, we knew, was to keep them in clear, fresh saltwater, **devoid** of sand and muck for a few hours, preferably overnight. In that manner, the shellfish effectively clean themselves out.

On the way back to my house I dropped off Tod, as he had a commitment to attend to with his family. Upon my arrival home, I immediately transferred my **succulent** morsels to our sideyard smoking/barbeque station. After I stoked up the fire, it wasn't long before my parents showed up from the grocery store and found our backyard engulfed in **savory** smoke. My dad is a sucker for seafood, and he immediately traded me a Heineken fresh from the bag for the first smoked mussel. Dad never had more than a six-pack on hand; to him, drinking was a social-occasion activity, not an event in and of itself.

The next morning I had a few errands to run in town, and I decided to take my "new car." I went outside, opened the driver's side door and was blasted backward by the **foulest** odor I had ever had the misfortune of encountering. That new-car smell was gone, replaced by what seemed to be a **fetid** combination of Armor All and ammonia.

I stepped back two paces and wondered what was going on. Then, I began to put two and two together. The car had gone back to the dealership twice, by the salesman's own admission, and I now **surmised** that it wasn't due to a lack of power, but rather because of the **insidiously noxious** odor **emanating** from the vehicle. "This is cool," I thought, preparing myself for a challenge worthy of my intellect.

Fiction in Red II

The first order of business was to open all four doors and the hatchback, and get myself out of "nose shot" of the car. Living where we did, six miles out of town, we had the luxury of breathing in real pine-scented air--without having to buy one of those little green trees to hang from the mirror. I distinctly remember thinking that it was a good thing we lived in the woods; otherwise, that stench would have prompted the neighbors to drive me out of town!

When I walked back to the car 10 minutes later, I was surprised to find that the odor was gone. **Bewildered** but **undaunted**, I decided to use my nose, and as gross as it may seem, I proceeded to sniff every square inch of the car. I checked the carpeting, the seats the doors. I peered into the headliners and under the visors, and poked around under the seats. Still, I couldn't come up with anything.

After nearly a half hour of sinus underload, I wondered if I was losing it. At that point, I was determined to find out if the smell would come back. I knew that my parents wouldn't pull a prank like that, but I considered that my sister and her friends just might, if they thought they could get away with it.

I went inside, fixed a sandwich, and then went back outside to my car. As I opened the door I found that the dreaded smell was back! Again I opened the doors, grabbed a patio chair, and sat down to face the problem with my mind. What would cause an ammonia smell like that? I then remembered a story I had read during my freshman

Eddy Ivy

Honors English class, which contained a passage about how efficient the Roman Empire was in exacting **revenue** from the general **populace**. One particular reflection was that the Roman rulers taxed the people who collected urine from the public urinals to make ammonia.

Then it hit me: No human would be inclined to urinate in a car, but a dog might!

I went to the hatchback and inspected the carpet. Aha, I found a hair. Light brown in color and short, it would have been easily missed on the dark-blue car carpet. I opened the spare tire compartment, but I didn't see or smell anything out of the ordinary.

There was only one thing left to do, I decided. I removed the bolt that secured the spare tire, and there, the cause of my **predicament** was uncovered at last. The area just under the spare tire was a low spot that had served as a collecting pool for almost a gallon of **putrid** yellow dog pee!

I then decided to sacrifice a pair of latex gloves. Placing my hand in the soup-like curd, I found and pushed out the rubber drain plug--standard in most cars' spare tire compartment. Then I hosed off the driveway and drove to the dealership in one of my alternate vehicles and ordered a new cargo rug for my "new" car.

Moral of the story: Those who fail to study history will never profit from it.

16
The 20-Foot-Tall Christmas Tree

I magine that you are 14 years old and live 6.2 miles out of town, in an unincorporated Oregon coastal hamlet named Glasgow, with a mere 275.5 residents. Wouldn't it be nice to have some kind of conveyance to get you out of the boonies and in to where the action always seemed to be, in the incorporated town of North Bend? My 10-speed bike was adequate, most of the time, but if the need arose to get somewhere fast, well, I was plain out of luck.

On a nice October day, I went out with my tireless dog for a long bike ride to town. The unusually warm water of the Pacific Ocean known as **El' Nino** was keeping the typically cold sheeting rains of mid-autumn at bay. The 8-mile bike ride had landed me at the Honda dealership. There, the sight of a glistening yellow-and-white moped caught my interest. The bare-bones vehicle was called the Hobbit, didn't need to be licensed, and was $349 dollars. The expenditure was just a hair out of the price range I was comfortable with at the time, as my savings-account balance was always a priority.

Eddy Ivy

Pulling up behind me on a scooter, a man asked, "Hey, son. Aren't you the wrestler who was in the paper a few weeks ago?" Turning around, the sight of a classmate's father, Mr. Harless, sporting a big grin, put me at ease. "You really put the hurt on young Mr. Hurt with that half nelson, young man. What's your name?"

Grinning from ear to ear, I responded candidly, "Yep, and my 15 minutes of fame will probably be over after the next meet, Mr. Harless. My name's Eddy, by the way."

He owned the Honda dealership franchise, so his next question, naturally, turned to my interests. "Well, I like this moped," I ventured cautiously, "but it is a little out of my price range."

Seeming uninterested in my financial challenge, Mr. Harless said, "Take it out for a test drive, Eddy," he said. Giving my dog the lay and stay command, I was off the lot in a minute. The Hobbit possessed a 50-cc engine that propelled me along pleasantly and reliably at about 30 miles an hour. Needless to say, I was hooked.

When I walked back in, Mr. Harless eyed me casually, and said, "Well, son, how did it handle?" The only thing I could think to say was "Great, just great!"

Then he asked what I might have for a trade-in. Jokingly, and looking down at my feet, I said, "Well, how about a **thoroughbred** Scottish terrier from Glasgow?" Knowing he was the topic of conversation, my mutt, Scotty, who would follow me anywhere, pulled himself to attention.

"OK, how about 50 bucks?" Mr. Harless said, to keep the conversation flowing. "Are you serious?" I asked, gasping a little at the thought. Mr. Harless softened then, and reassured me. "Eddy, I really don't want your dog, but it appears that you come in here a lot to look at the motorcycles," he said. "So, it's in my best interest to treat you well, since I'm sure you will keep coming back once I've earned your trust."

The next day was a sad day for my Scotty dog. I was thrilled with my new wheels, but the two-wheeled contraption was way too fast for him to keep up. It was also to be a sad day for me, though I didn't know it at the time. Over the course of the next month every cop in that coastal community pulled my yellow buzzing motorbike over at least once. Whether this occurred as a result of their curiosity, boredom, or just for fun, the mild harassment didn't subside until my complaints to a classmate, whose father was the chief of police, heard about my plight one night over dinner.

In my travels around the town, I frequently racked up 25 to 30 miles on any given day. The Hobbit proved durable, easy to push around off-road, and highly gas efficient. The only drawback was that there was only one gear for pedaling. This worked well enough when I was pedaling up 40-degree grades whenever I absentmindedly allowed myself to run out of gas. But aside from that, it was a waste even having the bicycle sprocket option, I realized.

Eddy Ivy

Several weeks after purchasing my new found freedom, I was out and about on one of those cold but dry December mornings. My travels included a stop at an old-time lumberjack café that boasted a 99-cent breakfast for any diner who purchased a cup of 50-cent coffee. It was worth the expense just to listen to the retired longtime loggers' stories. These guys had seen me often over the years, first with my father, and later, on my own, so it wasn't uncommon for me to join in the conversation at the counter and ask questions. Out of the blue, that day, I asked old Jack, who notoriously but **surreptitiously** added a shot of Jack Daniels to his coffee after each warmer, where I could find a good 20-foot Christmas tree near my house on the other side of the bay.

"Why do you want such a tall tree?" asked Barry, another patron. "Because we live in 27-foot-tall A-frame," I ventured, "and I want to surprise my parents." A younger man down the counter who I had never seen before chimed in, "Kid, if you go a mile up the water tower trail off Eastshore North, there might be some Douglas fir trees of that size!"

The dozen men in that smoke-filled greasy spoon immediately **erupted** in laughter. "Really?" I asked naively, not knowing what was going on. "You bet, Eddy," said Jack, "and if you get there before they log it again they probably won't mind a bit." Another round of laughter ensued. Not sure of what to make of this **ostensibly** one-sided conversation with a bunch of old farts, my errands in town started looking really appealing. I peeled myself of the counter stool, tipped the really cute waitress, paid my bill, and walked out.

Fiction in Red II

That evening I determined to prepare in advance for the next morning's tree hunt, as my curiosity was killing me. Wondering how I might use the Hobbit to aid in my quest, I quickly hatched a plan. After I had laid out a large plastic tarp, a good sturdy rope, and a medium-sized axe, I deemed my prep work done, without too much trouble. My plan was to get up early, go find a tree, cut it down, wrap it in plastic and tow it home behind the moped with a rope.

I arose at about 6:30 a.m. sharp and started on my mission as planned. Following the directions the fellow diner had offered the morning before proved to be an easy task; the only water tower known to me was located a short trip from my house. Proceeding up forest road No. 1976, the nice gravel side road turned into a narrow steep trail as soon as I passed the large holding tank.

Soon the trail began to close in on me, and the dew-laden brush flanking the trail was getting annoying. Getting wet had not been part of my plan, but giving up the mission and acknowledging failure was not becoming of me—especially as it had been only minutes since I left my house. Slowly creeping up the **unkempt** trail, the Hobbit was living up to its name. It wasn't a dirt bike, of course, but the mini-vehicle appeared to enjoy the challenge as much as I was, once the annoyance of becoming drenched had worn off. After awhile the trail ran **devolved** into a well-worn dirt bike trail. Finally able to pull back on the throttle, I felt a smile creep across my face. Then, as I passed the crest of the hill, a smirk **suffused** my mug. Looking out, I saw hundreds of thousands of Christmas trees, as far as my eye could see—and they were all roughly 20 feet tall!

Now I understood what had promoted the men's laughter, and I realized what Jack had meant. You see, when he said, "You need to get there before they log it again, Eddy," he was referring to the thinners, who would soon cull out all the excess trees.

Of course, no ordinary tree would do. I had to find the perfect tree! Parking my Hobbit underneath an extraordinarily large fir I set out to fulfill my mission. Wandering aimlessly I came upon a fenced off 12-foot-high-by-50-foot square barbed wire fence. Some sort of experiment or research project, I reasoned. Looking inside this fortress I saw the mother of all Christmas trees! It was perfectly formed and 20 feet tall.

The nerve of those researchers, I thought. Everyone knows that kids go out into the woods and occasionally cut down random trees for the fun of it. Their research data is going to be skewed if I don't go in there and cut at least one down. At least that was my reasoning at the time, if you must know!

Moral of the story: Never trust a kid with an axe!

17
The Backflip

When I was in high school and living on the Oregon coast we were able to choose among several electives in our **curriculum**. During my junior year I had an extra spot to fill, as I had taken driver's education the previous summer on my own time. Because I have always enjoyed making things, I decided to take wood-shop.

Before the teacher would let students loose in the shop, we, understandably, and fortunately for most of those around us, were required to demonstrate certain safety **competencies**. These included wearing proper eye protection, verbally explaining how to safely use all of the wood working machines, and making a half dozen standardized projects using only hand tools.

These competencies, despite the learning value they were intended to deliver, were actually an annoyance to me. I had grown up around wood lathes, band saws, planers, radial-arm saws, routers and a lot of other unconventional woodworking tools that our school didn't even possess.

Eddy Ivy

What I lacked for one project that I had always wanted to build, however, was a large quantity of clamps, the **requisite** space and a few extra pairs of hands.

With those at my disposal I resolved to build the biggest sand-board in the world. A standard sand-board is simply an old flat-bottomed water-ski, bisected, with a piece of Formica fastened to the bottom with contact cement. My idea was to make a ski-like board from scratch that was extra wide and extra long. This approach would increase the surface area touching the sand and, in theory anyway, increase the speed and carrying capacity of the craft.

More specifically, the blueprint I submitted resembled a short, wide toboggan featuring a very stiff suspension. Further modifications would give the contraption a much lower profile than that of typical waterski. It also sported a three-inch-high, triple-reinforced **bullnose** front and a slick **Formica** bottom.

My wood shop teacher, a man we pupils referred to as Mr. Blockhead, was not entirely convinced that I would be able to line up the two **Rabbet** "Z" shaped joints all the way down the middle of the two separate boards, and then match the forward curves of two different boards, and, finally, join them together perfectly.

To his utter amazement, I succeeded. My guess is that Mr. Blockhead didn't fully grasp what I was trying to accomplish, even though he had viewed the project sketches

I had drawn up in a separate drafting class. He likely failed to grasp the strength of the two-by-four bull-nose and the added strength conferred by the Formica sheet glued to the bottom, all of which my blueprint clearly included.

The sandboard worked like a charm. It was easily twice as fast, and would glide four times as far, as an ordinary short thin sandboard. An added bonus was the heavy-duty rope handle attached to both sides. That handle not only served to pull the **monstrosity** up a sand dune with ease but could also be attached to a rope, enabling someone to tow the board behind a sand buggy on the beach!

One particularly nice weekend in May when the temperature had reached a scorching 80 degrees I had met up with my good friend, Tod, and his younger brother, Brent, at a secluded but immensely popular place called Hall Lake. Besides being about 10 miles out of town, the trail to the lake was inaccessible except by foot. Those two attributes would have made the spot ideal for skipping school or throwing wild parties. But for some odd reason, no one in our class ever did that.

To get a sense of the area, picture a kidney-shaped, football field-sized lake. On the inner concave side it was forested by 70-foot **conifers**, which framed a small cove containing a 15-foot **cascading** waterfall that fed the lake. On the outer convex side it was flanked by a towering sand dune at least 100 feet high. By virtue of their sheer drama, the opposing landscapes, separated by the still, dark, black water, made for a scenically stunning destination. To add to the spot's allure, the dune side faced the warm southern sky and had an eight-foot **Berm**, which by the way, had a well-deserved reputation for attracting the latest swimwear fashions.

Once word got around about the speed of my monster sized sand-board, Brent asked if he could try out the thing. Distracted at that moment by one particular fashion show, I muttered, "Sure, Brent," and thought nothing more of it. Brent carted the board to the very top of the sand hill and started down, gaining speed up until he was hurtling toward the lake at a speed of at least 20 miles per hour. When he was almost halfway down, I realized, in a momentary **premonition**, what Brent was about to do. He wasn't going to go splashing right into the lake; he had aimed at the only clump of sea grass on the shoreline, situated at the dune's base! Knowing that he was going to attempt a jump didn't bother me; what concerned me was that I wasn't sure if he had scouted out the depth of the water he would be landing in!

Before Brent hit the jump, I had already had one of those **inklings** that something bad was about to happen. In fact, I was already on my feet and running toward the jump point before he hit the grassy hill. As everyone watched wide-eyed and speechless from the shore, within seconds Brent was flying 10 feet up in the air doing an unrehearsed backflip, courtesy of the steep angle of this unlikely jump ramp.

Fortunately, the water where Brent landed was deep. Had Brent not been propelled 10 feet out past the shores waterline, he would have landed in less than a foot of water Just as he plunged headfirst into the lake, I got there right behind him by using the grassy mound as a base to jump out to where he was coming up for air. I I tentatively ventured the only reasonable question one might ask: Are you OK, Brent?" Though visibly a little dazed, Brent uttered a weak "yes" and a nervous laugh.

The sand-board survived the trip reasonably intact as well, but by the time I collected myself, the thing had skipped almost halfway across the lake. I realized that I had better move quickly before it made its way downstream through an old sawmill's **sluice** box. Swimming out swiftly—OK, frantically, if the truth be told!--I seized and then pushed my prized sandboard back across the lake like a paddleboard.

Now, I wasn't crazy enough to go flying off that jump like my friend's younger and inexperienced brother had done. I had another plan. During my observation of the board skipping out across the water, I had wondered if it could possibly carry a rider out across the lake, and if so, how far. So far the splash had been no more dramatic than one a juvenile might make, and this type of macho spectacle was just about the normal scene of Hall Lake, at any rate.

Tugging the board onto the beach and then rubbing it down with the readily available hot sand to dry it off, I then applied paraffin wax on the Formica side to provide a slicker running surface. Then I excitedly carried the board up the dune, turned it around, and aimed for an area where the sand would allow for a far smoother, more gentle entry into the lake—the kind of level terrain one finds on a sandy beach just where the land meets the ocean. Before taking off, I wondered nervously if my idea would work.

Amazingly, seconds into my trip, I understood that I had pulled together the ideal combination of three specific features by mistake. My wide snow board design had just created a dual-purpose skim-board and sand-board specifically suited for sand dune lakes. There was no doubt now in my mind that it was going to work.

The extra speed gained from the added wax, the angle of entry, and my body position on the board were all perfect. When I hit the water, the board didn't "dig in" as I suspected it might. Instead, for the first 20 yards I actually skipped across the water. As my momentum decreased, I slowly began to sink, but not until I had traveled more than 80 feet across the lake.

Needless to say, friends, acquaintances and basically anyone who had heard the story or seen this big ride happen, lined up for the rest of the day and clamored to try the board, including my favorite fashion model.

Moral of the story: Most things in life have more than one use; the trick is to find the second one!

18
The Canadian Mist Trio

O ur high school history teacher, Mr. Omega, during our senior year, told our class that the Sixes River, just about 60 miles from our school, was once a well-known destination of adventure-seekers near and far. During the days of the Great Gold Rush, in the mid 1800's, even grade-school children, from coast to coast, knew the river by name. In fact, the Oregon Trail had been made famous in part due to this small stream, fabled to be rich with gold.

This short history lesson was enough to spur the imagination of my good buddy, Tod, and an outing seemed to be a promising antidote to "senioritis." Within days of learning about the Sixes, the combination of the lure of adventure and the soaring price of gold became too much for Tod to ignore, and he started formulating a plan. It didn't take long before the gold-digging bug bit me as well.

Tod and I purchased an old gold pan and headed down to the Sixes the following weekend, to try our luck. Our first trip down was almost a complete **washout**. We found a few flakes of the shiny stuff, which was enough to prompt us to come back again after doing a bit more research.

The second trip down wasn't much better. We found enough gold to almost fill one tenth of a one-tenth-ounce gold **vial** container. That really wasn't much to brag about, but we did anyway. By our third trip, we hit pay dirt and the gold bug had gotten us good.

Our achievement that hot July weekend was due largely to our strategic use of deductive reasoning. By digging out a hole in the side of an old overflow where the current had run roughly 100 years before, we were pleasantly surprised. We had succeeded in stumbling upon a **tier** of **sediment** which obviously hadn't been worked in the last 40 years. Over the course of three days, we managed to pan out a little more than one ounce of gold flakes and a few small nuggets.

Having developed a proven system, we became proficient panners and eventually decided that we needed to sell some of our gold so that we could afford our trips. It didn't take long before we had an eager buyer, a Cooston man who said he could sell our gleanings as scrap to a dental supply company for a better price than anyone else in the area would offer us. Even though the man was our dentist, we employed **due diligence** and always stopped by one of the local scrap dealers beforehand in order to check the weight of our booty. In this way, we were always sure of the fair market value of our gold before we sold it to our trusted friend.

Fiction in Red II

As our modest operation grew, we purchased a **sluice box** made specifically for gold and decided to bring in another laborer, our friend Jeff into the fold. Now a trio, we found ourselves winding up the Sixes River road in my tricked-out blue Chevy van, which we had determined was far better suited to sleeping three people than Tod's VW bus was. On a pullout on the outside of a gravel curve, a half dozen miles or so from Highway 101, we finally found a place that Friday night in May where we could we could safely pull off for the night.

Where the three bottles of Canadian Mist whiskey came from on that particular trip, I do not precisely remember. But as we weren't going anywhere in my van that night, the game was on. We had brought along a box of ginger snaps and a two-liter bottle of cola as a chaser. Snap, gurgle, pop in a clockwise rotation; that was the drill. This routine continued for about an hour, until we had finished our competition. We deemed it a three -way tie because we had run out of game pieces.

It seems that I have a very high tolerance for alcohol, so at the end of our game, it only took me 10 minutes to crawl up into the van's passenger-side captain's chair. One foot a minute isn't too bad for a first time drinking experience! Fortunately, as it turned out, I couldn't figure out how to adjust the seat back for a more comfortable snooze. This slight annoyance was due to the fact that I was always used to being in the driver's seat and couldn't find the seat latch due to my ever so slight **inebriation**.

Eddy Ivy

In my upright position I was kept awake for the most part. Looking out the window, I saw my buddies lying in the road in front of me. What few brain cells were actually working prompted my groggy body into slow motion.

Even though we hadn't seen a vehicle in the previous six hours, somehow I decided it would be a good idea to go pull them out of the road. At 138 pounds and able to lift 280 pounds when sober, I was stronger than I looked. So I reached down and grabbed Tod and Jeff by their shirt collars and dragged them, both at the same time, to the side doors of my van.

Afflicted as I was, I heaved them in as best I could and instantly regretted my action. The jostling was enough that both boys started **puking** all over the blue velour interior of my van. The smell was so **nauseating** that I almost **retched** myself, but by that point in the evening, all I really wanted to do was to crawl back up into my comfy captain's chair and go to sleep.

After I had finally adjusted the seat back and closed my eyes I was ready for a sound nights sleep. Somewhere between getting comfy and dozing off I sensed an **innocuous** illumination inside the van. Four seconds later, six blazing halogen fog lights began to fill our sanctuary. These piercing beams seemed to be ever increasing in brightness and immediately produced three drunken groans. A split second later, a logging tractor came whipping around the bend, going fast enough to lightly spray my van with gravel. Being in the front seat I realized that the driver had navigated the turn exactly in the portion of the road where my friends had just been lying.

I'm eternally grateful that the truck driver didn't come by five minutes sooner, and that I wasn't the only one to survive that night.

Moral of the story: Drink responsibly; better yet, volunteer to be a designated life-saver.

19
The Hungarian Work Dog

I met Sherri while spring skiing at Timberline Lodge in 2002. She was a cute little Brunette with a dry sense of humor which was a bit like mine. She had a new-found **passion** for skiing and was passionate about every aspect of skiing. That is par for the course for many **novice** ski bunnies who, once bitten, become **obsessed** with what's humorously defined as an expensive but legal form of powder addiction. For the remainder of the season, Sherri and I spent most of our spare time skiing together.

After the snow began to melt and spring skiing turned into rock hopping we spent less and less time together. Sherri had changed jobs and was finding that her new responsibilities included a lot of traveling. Not wanting to leave her dog "Lucky" home alone, she happily accepted my offer to render dog-sitter services.

The claim of Lucky's name and very **existence** was that he and his sister had been **abandoned** in the woods. Sherri and her sister just happened to come upon the two puppies while hiking in some low hills while on vacation in Hungary. Whether this was a true story I do not know, for to me, Lucky looked like an ordinary old skinny mutt. Whether or not he was a **mongrel** did not matter to me. His **affable** disposition wholly **circumscribed** what animal **magnetism** is all about. Another endearing attribute, which I found most agreeable, was that Lucky literally slept 23 hours a day, due to his advanced age.

Unfortunately, six months later Sherri was transferred to California and, you guessed it, I got Lucky. All of this was happening at the time when I was remodeling a house in Portland that had been a rental for 18 years. The carpets, left over furniture and drapes, had been removed immediately when I bought the house for inescapably **odorous** reasons. This subtraction of **chattels**, so to speak, made my decision to take in Lucky much easier. Sherri had gone on almost *ad nauseam* about Lucky's intelligence—a **mantra**-like ramble that I had chalked up to her love for the dog.

And I loved him, too—especially when I found out how easy it was to train him. One day Lucky was caught in the act lifting his leg. Running over and admonishing him with a sternly spoken "no!" I dragged his 50-pound frame over to the third bedroom. Just inside the door, I had set up an old waterbed liner for just such an emergency. When Lucky finally "went," I **commended** him **profusely**, and from then on that is where he did his **"whizness"** if I wasn't at home. He was also already very good at getting up, going to the door, and barking profusely to let me know that it was time to fertilize my lawn when I was home.

About a month after Sherri left town, I finally ran out of the specially **formulated** dog food that Lucky nibbled on throughout the day. Since he was now my dog, and I really didn't feel **compelled** to spend $80 for a bag of specially formulated dog food, I drove to a canned food discount outlet and bought several different varieties of pet food to see which he would like best.

I grabbed three small bags of different brands of dry food, and three one-pound containers of different brands of canned dog food. I felt confident that Lucky would like at least one or two of the selections. When I got home, I laid out all six varieties in a **smorgasbord**-like arrangement on the floor. I then went over to Lucky and coaxed him up with a Rolled Gold pretzel, which was about the only thing he would get excited about those days. Walking over to the six bowls of food, he stopped, looked up at me, and tilted his head to the right, as if to say, "Are you OK, Eddy? Then he started sniffing each pile of food. I noticed that he really had to work at it, that is, until he made his way to the one-pound can of food that had been on sale for the ridiculously low price of 10 for a dollar.

What happened next amazed me. Lucky appeared to change **species**, as he began pigging out, in the literal sense. Within a few seconds, he had **snorted** the whole lot down and then looked up at me, endearingly, as if to ask, "May I have some more of this delicious food, kind sir?"

Joyfully picking up the can, I couldn't help but to say aloud--"What a bargain!"—as a big smile crept over my face. Further inspection of the label on the can he had just **scarfed** down revealed that it was not dog food but rather a large can of cat food. Thinking back to his initial sniff test a few moments earlier, and the fact that Lucky loved salty pretzels, it occurred to me that he must have been losing some of his sense of smell; that explained his lack of **appetite**.

From then on, mixing up a little dry dog food and a half can of "intoxicatingly fishy" cat food became the new breakfast routine I performed before I went off to work. I repeated the act for Lucky's dinner when I got home, and found that this **regimen** made him gain weight like a fryer on corn feed. He still slept 23 hours a day and would only move for a pretzel or the promise of a road trip.

That dog loved to go to Home Depot, that **Mecca** for the do-it-myself home-improvement crowd. He must have had some previous experience because he would instinctively climb up onto a flat cart and arrange his body in to a **stoic** Egyptian **sphinx** position. His **docile** yet friendly face got him lots of compliments and plenty of attention. Everybody who liked dogs would just come up out of the blue and start petting him without worry about being bitten. Lucky would eat it up, knowing that he could pant faster and get more attention and then give out a little whine as they were leaving as if to say, "please come back!" I found that even the **imminent** danger of being crushed by supplies I needed to place on the cart wouldn't cause him to move. He had an **immanent** understanding, surely, that I wouldn't hurt him.

One evening as usual I came home and let Lucky go outside before starting dinner. He did his business quickly, as it was raining heavily. I cleaned up the dishes and he went over to his favorite spot five feet in front of the fireplace, curled up on his pillow bed and went to sleep as usual. I turned off the lights and left the **spacious** grand room to its master.

After brushing my teeth and starting in on some neglected chores I heard what had appeared to be a slamming door or some object falling hard. I knew something was wrong, so I walked **stealthily** down the hall and out to the grand room-- where I found Lucky still asleep but, the lights were on full blast! I went over to the door and found four footprints. Two were facing inward and the other two were exiting. Evidently some ill-intentioned person had found my door open, turned on the lights, and decided not to stick around to deal with Lucky who was now weighing in at about 80 pounds.

The would-be burglar must have felt a movement in his shorts, but for the wrong reason. You see, even though Lucky wouldn't have hurt a fly even if he had been capable of catching one, I had had been in the other room cleaning and reloading my three handguns.

Moral of the story: Let sleeping dogs lie.

20
The Turd Bird That Hated Men

S ummer break of my junior year at Southern Oregon State University had been a myriad of mini and Miss-adventures. Initially I had spent a couple of weeks exploring long forgotten hiking trails around Crater Lake. According to a little bird, these **unkempt** trails had been long abandoned by the Forest Service due to lack of funding. Next I had to meet up with my parents in Honolulu for a week; heck it was their dime, so I figured why not! The fact that they looked like the typical tourists dressed in flowered birds-of-paradise adorned Hawaiian shirts, virtually irremovable leis and classic plaid shorts was comforting for a change, only because that was what everybody in Honolulu was wearing!

That week was probably the best week I had spent with my parents ever. I had managed to score a new wardrobe, see a lot of exciting shows, eat great food, and actually get a bird's eye view of them relaxing for a change. Since I had kept in contact with a cross-country team member who lived in Maui, I wasn't too surprised by an invite to spend an extra week or so with him.

Eddy Ivy

Upgrading my return ticket was handled by my parents, and before I knew it the phrase "a wing and a prayer" came to mind while viewing the tiny wings of a very small Cessna vibrate while we were heading for Maui. Joe and his parents were more than gracious hosts, and the week turned into what seemed more like a month! I could have stayed longer but the cost of upgrading my return ticket every week got old fast! Soon I found myself at PDX praying that the battery in my Chevy Cavalier had held a starting charge for its extended **furlough**.

Arriving home I found it empty. It turned out that my parents and sister were in Montana doing a little work on the family farm. Solitude suited me fine for the moment; aside from mowing the grass, saying hi to the neighbors, cleaning the fish pond and getting my now senile 19 year old Scotty dog out of hawk from the local kennel. Upon my parents return I was immediately off to Ashland. Over the phone I had arranged to work at my favorite Pizza Shack part time and stay with my High School buddy Craig for a couple of days.

As luck would have it I was able to confirm my employment at Pizza Shack immediately by working four hours on the clock. Watching the diesel plumes of an unannounced three-bus tour group leaving the parking lot I arrived at the restaurant at precisely the right moment. I was able to proof a couple of fresh batches of dough for the normal night rush, restock the entire salad bar, and **begrudgingly** washed all of the dishes and pans. I don't know who was more relieved, the manager (Tony) or me.

Fiction in Red II

Securing a guaranteed schedule of 20 hours a week was relatively easy, as Tony really needed someone who could do the books, be trusted with the keys, wasn't a flight risk, and could do the close a couple of nights a week. On my way to Craig's with a large pepperoni pizza, Tony handed me a bank bag, asking if I could make a drop on my way. The early bank deposit was for the benefit of the new waitresses, who had no idea who I was or why I was allowed to be working in my street clothes, **mullet** and all. "See you on the 27th," I replied.

Making the drop, I chugged up to Craig's pad ready to chow down on a dinner of gratitude; compliments of Tony. Opening the passenger side door of my truck to get the large pizza I was startled by a bird that landed on my right shoulder. I looked and saw that it was a mid-sized green parrot. And he wasn't going anywhere! Knocking on the door to Craig's place I cried out "pizza delivery," and walked inside. The place was full of friends, as usual, and I realized that my share of half the pizza would immediately go down to only a couple of slices.

"What's up with the bird?" someone asked. I replied, "I don't really know--it just landed on me outside. I think someone accidentally lost him." Just then Tracy came out of the bathroom, and immediately the parrot flew over to her and started cooing, and wouldn't leave her.

She asked if she could keep him, to which I replied, "I'd rather go to Goodwill and get a cage and some food, and try to find the owner. Besides," I said, "If you lost Mr. I-wanna-be-a-feather-duster in my next life, wouldn't you want someone to at least try to find you?"

"No," she said, focusing her puppy-dog eyes on me. "OK," I said. "I'll make you a deal. If no one claims Mr. Dusty, then you can have him."

Satisfied that she had won the discussion, she went back to feeding him some sunflower seeds, and I went off to Goodwill. There I found a nice big blue cage for $20. Recounting my tale, I was told I that could return it for a full refund if I found the owner within 30 days. Fortunately, there had been multiple cages and supplies on hand, and the manager gave me almost 50 pounds of feed for free. This amount was actually all of the bird feed in the store, which she said would eventually go bad since they were a mixture of pre-opened packages and bags.

I spent the night, went home to the coast, and traded my truck for my Chevy Cavalier station wagon, now fully loaded with new school clothes. Returning to my newly rented house, I unloaded my belongings and went over to Craig's place to say hello. Looking around I noticed that the bird and the cage were was gone. "So, did you **succumb** to Tracy's whining?" I joked. "No, Eddy," he replied. "We actually found the owner, and Tracy's boyfriend wouldn't let her keep it anyway!"

I looked puzzled. "What are you talking about?" I said.

In the five years that I had known her, starting back in high school, Tracy would get whatever Tracy wanted. "It's the weirdest thing, Eddy," Craig said. "You see, that bird just hates guys for some reason--and the only male the bird hadn't attacked was you!"

After obtaining the address of the gal who had claimed the bird, I excused myself and went off to get the big blue cage. Craig said she had promised to bring it back immediately, but so far, no one had see or heard from her. Releasing the mullet from my Los Angeles Dodgers baseball cap, I thought to myself, I know a good study for my bird-brained biology teacher who gave me a B in **ornithology**.

Knocking on the door at the address of the bird's owner, I was pleasantly surprised by a room full of women. Introducing myself as the guy who found the parrot, I was slightly taken back when an **uncouth** woman asked in sneering tone, "What do you want?" Looking around the room, I was amazed that her friends appeared unaffected by her rather rude demeanor. Straight away, I remembered that old **adage** that birds of a feather flock together, and decided not to gander.

In a low tone, I replied, "Just the blue cage, please. " Then she asked in an ill-mannered manner and high pitch, "What are you going to do with it?" Producing a slightly wrinkled receipt for my $20 expenditure, I said, "The Goodwill store manager said they would return my money if I found the owner of the parrot." Thrusting the blue cage at me without the slightest hint of a thank you, she then slammed the door in my face. At that point I actually felt sorry for the bird, but I felt comforted knowing I had done the right thing.

Moral of the story: Although you may regret sticking to your principles at times, at least your friends will know where you stand.

21

Tour De Phoenix Narrative

In Phoenix, Arizona, there's not a whole lot to do when you are only 15 years old and you know you'll only be there during the summer break from school. That summer, a new friend, Jeff, called up and told me that we could go on an adventure if I could scrape up a few bucks and show up at his place at 9 a.m. wearing cut-offs. Being new to the area--and bored stiff--I jumped at the opportunity.

At 9 o'clock sharp, Jeff met me on his front doorstep. He refused to tell me where we were going. The only clue he gave me was that our destination was an unbelievable "paradise."

"You'll love it, Eddy!" he pronounced. "It's unbelievably cool." Crossing my eyes and making funny face, I said, coolly, "Yes, and how so?"

"Well, there are palm trees, and there's a huge pool and great waterslide," Jeff said. "Oh, and I forgot to mention yesterday, lots of girls our age, too!" The last part would have sufficed for me at that point. There were a quite a few extremely good-looking "women" that frequented the pool at our apartment, but no girls our age.

Still, at this point in time, my **inclination** was to disbelieve everything he said and promised. After all this was Phoenix, then a city of more than one million people, and as far as I could tell, it was the epitome of the stench of civilization. There were a few watered lawns and an occasional palm tree, but compared to the Pacific Northwest, it was, in my not-so-humble view, a **barren**, waterless, arid maze.

Still, I was up for anything that would break the monotony that morning. So we hopped on our gorilla hanger-handlebar five-speed bikes, which resembled "California Cruisers," and headed out with Jeff assuming the lead.

Our movement, graceful and sure, was like that of crafty pawns on a chessboard. We carefully veered in and out of traffic, navigating up and down streets, and took pride in finding short cuts through parking lots, en route to our adventure.

About a half hour into our journey, we weaved through a passel of small children trying to fry an egg on the hot black alley's pavement, while a little brown dog greedily licked his chops in anticipation. My newfound buddy didn't seem to mind this home-spun spectacle or the heat; it was a mere 95 degrees as measured by the bank's rotating display sign. Jeff had, in fact, chuckled at my first complaint 10 minutes earlier. "Eddy, don't you realize that it's still cool out? Just wait until 4 p.m.," he said. "Then you can tell me about hot!"

Sweating like a stuck pig turning above a barbecue pit, I asked, "How can it get any hotter than this?" Jeff laughed, and said, "For starters, you are going to be sunburned to a crisp by the end of the day. Point two: You probably won't save any money for pop on the way home. And point three, Eddy, is that I'm going to force you to lead the way home!"

Interrupting his gleefully **sadistic sarcasm** I ventured, loudly, "Dude," wiping my brow with the top of my T-shirt. "You're *used* to 90 degrees in the shade. But where I come from, when it hits 80 degrees outside, people start having heart attacks! If we don't stop to take a soda break now, they are going to donate my body to science as an exhibit of an example of **dehydration**!"

So we stopped at a Taco Bell. Sitting in the shade of a huge umbrella, we were amused by a drunk who was bumping into garbage cans and parking meters. Finally he found refuge on a bus stop bench and passed out cold.

Minutes later, we were off again on our bicycles—slowed somewhat by the molten tar that had gathered on our tires. As we reached what seemed to be the outskirts of the city, we passed dry gray buildings and crumbling brick apartments. The area had the appearance of being a place where the desert metropolis's less than well-heeled inhabitants toiled behind doors in nameless "light industrial" complexes and lived out their evenings in their baking **abodes**.

Looking at Jeff I knew that he knew that we were not in a good neighborhood. Speeding up slowly as if not to appear bothered by the local transients, all he could say at that point was "Hey, wait up for me!" Since this neighborhood was not trying to impress visitors with the richness of its quality of life I had decided to preserve mine; all I had to do was outrun Jeff. Advancing onward, we left the city slum behind us and peddled on a straight single road that was eerily like a vacant corridor in the desert floor leading to infinity. It was like that classic perspective drawing tool, the one that shows the rails of a train track coming together in the distance. After awhile, I felt like we were at the end, scissoring down the ridge of a sharp knife, death on either side of us, streaming past the gloating cacti and listless lizards sizzling on the flat rocks.

Rising in the distance, an oasis seemed to emerge. It was the perfect duplicate of a living **mirage** that some dying desert wanderer, days without water and crawling along on his hands and knees, would see. Jeff then revealed that it was not a mirage. We were heading toward "Big Surf," Arizona's answer to any coastal beach.

Entering at the front of the amusement park, we paid our admission at the ticket booth. On the way to the man made beach, we made our way past the showers, a hot dog stand, and the air mattress and surfboard rental areas.

On reaching the "beach," I gasped. Layered palm trees sprouted from the sand and swayed slightly in the hot desert breeze. These formed a stately hedge of sorts, and ran parallel to a formidable outline. This, I guessed, was really a fence to prevent trespassers. In the back of this three-acre man-made lake, a wall worthy of a high-security prison towered 50 feet in height.

Inside this back wall was the marvel which sustained this paradise. A monstrous wave-making mechanism produced six- to eight-foot cresting mountains of water, while a massive pump spewed the **requisite** water for a very long water slide.

Like eager souls escaping from hell, we plunged into the cool breaking waves with our rented air mattresses. We rode the waves wildly, calling out to each other every few minutes, for approximately half an hour, when our total glee was broke, startlingly, by the ominous ringing of a very loud bell. When I, dismayed, questioned why everyone was getting out of the water, Jeff replied, "It's the surfers' turn for awhile. Everybody else has to either watch them, or go ride the water slide."

Jeff was surprised when I reached into my soggy wallet and extracted a few extra bucks to rent a surfboard. I explained that, while in Oregon, I had learned to surf somewhat **proficiently**, in an environment that was a whole lot less predictable than the waves here at Big Surf! Throughout the compressed time limit, I thrashed the waves on my board, riding up and down the symmetrically cresting walls of water. Every three minutes another perfect wave came and I would catch it oh-so-effortlessly in a graceful manner that most "surfing" Arizonans, I suspected, would never master.

After a while, most of the guys who clearly spent a whole lot of time at Big Surf stopped, pulled their board onto the "shore," and simply watched me in awe. Jeff, for his part, sat there speechless.

In retrospect, I suppose that those surfers were just trying to figure out how to **emulate** my style. For me, the whole show was about showing up a lot of older guys and actually getting some attention from some of the girls we had met. Trying to act cool came to an end when we had to leave at closing.

Jeff made good on his earlier "threats" and my first problem was that I had to lead the way home. Leaving the oasis I decided to take a different route which seemed to make sense to me. Instead of weaving in and out of the city grid in a zigzag pattern I chose to move like a knight. Two miles up and three miles down; that was my plan for getting home. Jeff dutifully followed and after three miles I rode into a familiar Farrell's ice cream parlor.

Looking at me out of quizzical amusement, he said, "What are you doing? You don't have enough money left to buy a soda?" I looked back, and said. "Jeff, I have a nickel,

and rumor has it that they have two-cent soda water here."
"Yuk," he said. "I've had that before, and it tastes terrible!
Have you ever stirred in the free sugar packets?" I asked,
grinning.

Moral of the story: Never take a newcomer for granted.

22
Trail in the Sky

The seventh grade may seem a little late in **adolescence** to be building a tree fort, but my good friend, John, and I decided to go ahead and construct one anyway. My parents had just finished building an addition to our house, so we had plenty of lumber on hand, and long summer days to fill.

After considerable discussion, John and I decided that the best location for our fort would be in three sturdy alders. These stout trees were 60 feet high, and towered 20 feet higher than the cascara trees surrounding them. They were well hidden from the main road, and except for the distance from the ground, were fairly safe to climb as far as trees go.

The reason we chose this location was three-fold. The first was that a 90-foot Sitka spruce tree would hide our fort from my mom's prized view of the **estuary** and North Bend Bridge. The second was that the stand of alders was nearly halfway between John's house and mine. The third was that the spot was situated in a swampy **wetland** area. This made for a nice moat, which we would put to good use eventually.

As we had nearly 16 full sheets of three-quarter-inch plywood with 30-pound felt roofing, we decided to go all out and build a double-decker tree fort. To transport the 70-pound sheets to the base of our trees, we created a skinny wooden plank trail made out of 2 x 6's. This **rudimentary** bridge used any solid point in the swamp, including but not limited to stumps, branches, and even one very large **skunk cabbage**. This worked very well, but as you may well imagine, occasionally one of us would falter, slip in to the grime, and end up very wet, muddy and smelly.

We drew up no formal plans for the place, but we were determined to make our dream a reality. The base we came up with was a stroke of genius, we thought. The structure itself wasn't nailed into the trees, but instead was formed using 2-by-6s on top of the branches. The frame itself was nailed together to form a platform, but we used rope to secure it and to make the platform secure. We had come up with the idea that if we didn't use any nails, we wouldn't harm the trees and our structure would last a very long time.

The most distinctive **peculiarity** of our fortress was that the tree trunks themselves were all inside the structure. The area around the base of the trunk was cut slightly away from the trunk. This afforded us an excellent view of any of our rivals snooping around, who had their own tree forts elsewhere in the neighborhood. These pesky rivals were two years behind us in school. Ben and Jerry always wanted to tag along and copy whatever we were making or doing. I suppose we should have been flattered, but it's nice to have pests to swat from time to time if you know what I mean. So we were always trying to find new and creative ways to frustrate them.

We often succeeded in frustrating other people as well. Many times—well, actually most of the times while we were at our fort--we had fallen off our treacherous trail while making our way through the swamp and had often come home muddy. Our mothers urged us, begged us actually, to build a better trail.

We had plenty of time on our hands, so we leisurely started thinking about how to approach this new project. One idea had been to make a string of ropes like the vines in all of the Tarzan movies, but this brilliant solution, in the end, only served to make our spills even more **horrendous**.

Then we surmised that perhaps we could use rope to build a trail in the treetops. We had plenty of rope from a variety of sources we'd uncovered, so we experimented on two trees low to the ground, to see if our idea would work. We found that we could tie off the rope at the area where a branch came out from the trunk and then tie it off to the next tree.

It became evident that we would need two ropes on all of the spans over four feet long because of the sway factor. One rope would be for our hands, the other for our feet. We spaced one above the other at about four feet, and were soon convinced that it would be a safe way to get to the tree house.

We agreed that the best way to make our trail would be for John to go up one tree while I **scaled** the next one. Each of us would take our own rope, and begin our painstaking process of building our trail in the sky. Our first task was to decide where to start the trail.

Because our houses were separated by a small but steep gully with a small stream in the bottom which separated the properties, we decided on a T-shaped trail. That way John could exit his house on one side of the 20 foot gully and I could do the same on the other side.

The first part of our trail would create the pathway from John's house to mine. This first **endeavor** would be the top part of our T-trail. This part was also the easiest, as the trees were so dense that we didn't have to climb up and down each one in order to tie off each rope; we simply swayed the trees and grabbed hold of the next. We were finished within a day, largely due to the fact that we were able to start the trail at ground level to go across the gully. Also, as most of the trees were about the same age, the height of the branch tie-offs from tree to tree were all fairly level.

The second part of our trail was a little more difficult, as the trees were of widely differing ages and sizes, and were spaced as far as 10 feet apart. Each tree in this section of the trail had to be scaled. Then we realized that we had an additional problem; we didn't have the ability to make a level trail, or the luxury of a gully and symmetrical trees that would enable us to start off at ground level and go straight across to the other side.

Puzzling over our **conundrum**, we eventually decided that we might be able to climb up a few feet to get to the next section of branches for a solid, secure tie-off area. Our trail resembled a route that a knight on a three-dimensional chessboard might take by the time it reached the tree fort.

After we had finally completed our trail it was fun to call on the phone and race to our fort. Sometimes we actually met in the middle and argued who would get to take the fort section of the trail first. Little John usually won but Red robin Hood was always close behind.

Since we didn't want any visible entry, the last leg of our trail turned out to be a dangler. We simply used a single branch. Traversing hand over hand, our feet hanging, we would "land" on a 2" x 8" platform we had placed on the opposite outside wall of where the door was located.

With no visible means of entry this highway 16 feet up turned out to be an advantage in keeping the ice cream twins away from our fort that we had not thought about. For weeks, none of our adversaries had any idea hot to get to our fort once we took out our **precarious** wooden trail from the muddy swamp.

Moral of the story: New innovations often have beneficial side effects.

23
Two-Step Tiptoe

For the short time it was open, the Rocking Rodeo in Portland, Oregon, was a great place to hang out. It was one of those instant hot spots that only had a few months of flame before it smoked out into oblivion. Aside from the occasional drunken idiots getting into fights and being hauled off to jail, it was a lively spot. The ambiance of the western saloon style bar was only exceeded by the atmosphere of city slickers dressing up and pretending to be cowboys and cowgirls. Fortunately for the crowds, the primary format of the dance called the two-step was relatively easy to master.

One warm Friday night in July the Rocking Rodeo got a little too "hot." The kitchen actually caught fire and everyone including me had to be ushered outside by the fire department. It was in the parking lot that I met Vanessa. She had a fantastic personality, a mischievously beautiful smile and long fiery red hair, which probably started the fire in the first place.

After making small talk about the fire, she casually mentioned that she needed a ride home. During the brief half-mile ride to her apartment complex, the fine art of chit chat had paid off. We had a date for the next day. I wrote down her phone number and of course her apartment number, and took off.

The next morning I showed up on my Yamaha Virago with a spare helmet. She eyed the spare helmet in my hand warily while standing on her doorstep, and asked if the motorcycle had a sissy bar, since the bike was out of view in the parking lot. It turned out that she had promised her father years before that she wouldn't get on a bike without a backrest. After assuring her that it did, we went off to brunch at the Original Pancake house, just blocks from my place. At my suggestion—urging, actually, we ordered two of the Tahitian Maiden's Dreams **crêpes**, a delectable **concoction** of apricots and a secret creamy filling.

There is nothing, absolutely nothing, like the rush of pure sugar to get you going, and that is exactly what we did for the rest of the day. The first stop was at the Japanese Garden atop Marquam Hill. If you want to know an age old secret, the investment of a well-placed penny in the **Koi** pond will probably get you that first kiss. If you play your cards right you might even get two, if you tell your date that your wish was only half fulfilled. Then we were off to the famous International Rose Test gardens, which is only about 100 yards down the hill.

Fiction in Red II

Walking through the gardens there are hundreds of different varieties to look at. From primroses to the classic long-stemmed variety heavily purchased on Valentine's Day, if you like roses they have roses! Walking hand in hand on a path dedicated to Portland's historical Rose Festival queens, Vanessa playfully asked me which rose was my favorite. After immediately replying that she was, she laughed, and said, "No, I mean which flower?" I then took her up to my personal favorite, the Fragrant Cloud. Of course, on the way to the bush there was another opportunity to toss more copper, but you probably knew that was coming.

By 5 p.m. Vanessa and I had gotten to know each other fairly well; we were closing in on becoming borderline **famished**. She happened to know a nice little place across town called Gustav's that featured good German food. We were early, so we received very personalized service, as the regular dinner crowd didn't start showing up until about 6 p.m. We ordered the best roast duck I have ever eaten in my life, which was complemented by my favorite wine, a reasonably priced German brand called Liebfraumilch.

Midway through our meal, I disclosed that I had an important but **clandestine** operation that I had to do that evening, and that it required that I dress up in black and not go out until dark.

Looking at me like I was crazy, she gave me the I-give-up look and asked, "Well, Eddy, just what is it that you must do tonight?"

"It's a little dangerous, Vanessa," I ventured. "But if you promise not to tell anyone, I'll trust you with my cloak-and-dagger Mission Impossible task." She vowed to comply, and I continued, "You must understand that seven lives are at risk. Are you sure you're still in?"

Starting to appear a little worried, she said, in a small voice, "Yeah, um, sure, Eddy."

I described my mission. I told her that my goldfish were outgrowing my 10-gallon fish tank and needed a new home. "If they don't find a new place to live soon," I explained, "they may be caught up in a giant whirlpool leading to an ocean of unfriendly brown trout.

"We need to save them by sneaking them to a large goldfish sanctuary where they will be safe from the tidybowl man who has a license to kill," I continued. "So would you like to come with me?"

Laughing, she told me she had to go to the ladies room. To which I replied, "Well, the fish aren't here, you know. They're back at my place." Not long afterward, we were back at my house, where we got to know each other a little better while watching my fish eat the last of their fish flakes. Watching the laborious proceedings, Vanessa said that she understood why the fish really needed a new home. "After all, who actually has the time or money to go out and buy fish food all of the time?" she offered.

Fiction in Red II

The time had come to get into the mood of the mission. We took up the code names of Boris and Natasha, and placed our contraband in a large coffee can. The trip was a short trip of about a mile away but still too far to walk with our cargo. Parking my car about a block away from our destination we got out like spies on a mission. I must say we fit in on that Baptist schools grounds campus fairly well. That is, until we saw a security guard walking toward us.

He was ambling slowly across the large campus that housed our small-fry lake coming directly for us! Fortunately for us, the guard merely glanced at us briefly and walked on by. I surmised that when a young man has a beautiful woman on one arm, "officials" rarely go to the trouble to ask why the guy has a can of coffee in the other.

Reaching the sea of opportunity, I felt a deep sense of relief that my old roommates would have a great new life ahead of them. Opening the tight lid I knew that my fish were safe at last—or soon would be, in any event. Gently releasing the swimmers into the pond, I nervously glanced upward, and joked with Vanessa. "Do you see any stray fish eagles?" I asked in a worried tone, but using silly voice that received a howl of laughter.

Then, somewhat ceremoniously, I turned toward Vanessa and looked deeply into her eyes. Reaching into my pocket, which was full of pennies, I took out one, and gently pressed it into her hand. In a feigned, very deep Russian accent, I said, "Comrade, make a wish. I'll try my best to make it come true!"

Moral of the story: Invest your pennies wisely!

P.S. Do not throw pennies in the KOI pond! Use a more secluded one!

24
Up in Smoke

Do you remember the first time you ever lit off a firecracker? My first experience was on July 4, 1973. My grandfather, Art, had bought me a brick of explosive sticks appropriately named Black Cats. I was **ecstatic** when he presented them to me, after all, they were, and remain to this day, the best firecrackers ever produced. They were larger than the average run-of-the-mill fireworks, had a little longer fuse and generally delivered a lot more bang for the buck. And as he had purchased an astonishing brick of 500 sticks, the kinds of fun an 11-year-old boy might come up with was almost endless, in my view.

My use, initially, was limited primarily to blowing up plastic soldiers, ant hills, Hot Wheels trucks that were lacking one or more wheels, and scaring the neighbor's cat. I engaged in the latter because that cat had gotten the idea that my grandmother's garden was her own private litter box. Using Black Cats to turn real cats into scaredy cats soon became our family's new prank of the week.

Eddy Ivy

A few days later, when the last of the scorching Fourth of July festivities were over, in any event, the novelty of discovering the Black Cats' **myriad** of uses was starting to wear off. The heat of the burning streets had forced me to play in the shade of our garage. In the back alley no Stray Cats were to be found, at least not in Glasgow, Montana. Up until that time, I had shared my precious new toy in a very limited fashion. In fact, the only one I had decided to let into my fireworks fold was my best friend, Robbie.

That changed a few days later, when a couple of neighbor boys from up the street came over to play. They had heard through the **grapevine** that "someone on our block had firecrackers." John and James made it clear that they would really like to be included in some of the fun, as their parents didn't buy them any for the holiday.

Within a few minutes we all found out why John and James parents wouldn't buy them any. In addition to lighting them whenever and wherever they chose—not to mention throwing them, lit, near anybody in proximity--one of the **miscreants** even stuffed a lit one in his brother's back pocket and it went off! When our little friend started crying and ran off in agony yelling for his mother, my unlimited sharing of my stash stopped--instantly. Of course, you can just imagine the irate phone call my grandmother received about a half-hour later. Even though the boy hadn't been hurt, his parents were so upset about the incident that they insisted that the reckless use of my firecrackers had to be stopped. The ensuing decision actually resulted in punishing me! I was informed, in one of those all-serious sit-down sessions that accompany such pronouncements, that my mini-sticks of dynamite would be taken away because I had supplied a dangerous weapon to a couple of complete idiots.

After dinner, my 79-year-old grandfather took what was left of my prized gift and said, "Come on, Eddy, let's go for a walk." He stood there on the cement porch in his every day cloths, typical of what you would expect of a World War 1 Veteran. It consisted of a classic white short-sleeved shirt, gray slacks ironed with a single line down the front, black socks, and his well worn wing-tip shoes. I knew we were up to an exciting adventure of some sort, but I wasn't quite sure of what it would be.

Smoking his Swisher Sweet cigar with his right hand, as he had done for decades, and holding my cats in his left hand, we were off to the race track! He slowly ambled beside me as we walked two blocks down to the Glasgow fairgrounds. After we crossed the street to enter the sandy horse track, my grandfather slowly withdrew the strip of firecrackers from the original cellophane package. It came out like an accordion picked up from one end since the fuses had been braided together at the factory. He then laid out the string of approximately 300 powder-packed noisemakers in the sand.

Lighting them off with his brown smoking **punk**, he stood back, folded his arms and, stood there with his cigar in his mouth unsupported by his hand. It struck me odd as I had never seen him do that before. Observation had always been one of my strong points and emulating him at that point was impossible. Like a stone he didn't move, no fidgeting, blinking or otherwise, and except for the smoldering stream of smoke from the end of the Swisher Sweet he was like a statue. We stood there and took in the sizzling show. The erratic sound was fast and furious almost like the gallop of hooves that rounded the track on race days. The sand was being thrown up as if there were actual horses charging out the starting gate. But the best part was the flashing blinks of light, which reminded me of the blazing eyes of horses one would see in pictures of western battle scenes.

Watching that string of crackers going off was like watching quarter horses going around that track. For the next 30 seconds the intensity was so overwhelming that I couldn't say a word. After it was all over we just looked at the spot where a small battle had just been fought. Dumbstruck, all I could think to say was, "Wow, that was cool, Grandpa!" Then it hit me that there were no more Black Cats, and my excitement quickly **waned**.

Walking the two short blocks in silence was probably too much for him to bear, since the firecrackers had been his gift to me. For some reason, out of that silence, he decided to confide in me. "Eddy, I've always wanted to live to be 80 years old and now, since I'm already 79, I think I'm going to make it," he pronounced gravely. Confused by what he was saying, I simply asked, "When is your birthday?"

Fiction in Red II

"It's December 10th," he said, as we walked back into the house to the welcoming scent and the real prospect of diving into a hot apple pie that hadn't been ready to eat earlier. That was the end of the conversation.

Late in the afternoon on November 10, I could tell that there was something wrong at my grandparent's house. My mother and grandmother were fussing over my grandfather and I was told to stay in the living room. Minutes later, an ambulance arrived and took my grandfather away to the hospital. Following a few minutes later in our car, my dad and I arrived at the hospital. I remember watching my mother holding my grandfather's hand through the glass partition and pressing her other hand up against her head. His lungs had totally given out from years of smoking, and his heartbeat got slower and weaker. Within a couple of minutes of our arrival he had died right there in front of me. I looked up at my father, who was holding my hand at the time, and perhaps not knowing what else to do just then, he looked down at me and said, "If he wouldn't have been a smoker, Grandpa would have made his 80th birthday next month."

Recalling his words from the 4th of July, I promised myself right then and there, that I would never smoke.

Moral of the story: Some gifts are priceless.

25
Wizard Island

When I was in my late teens, having time and money at my disposal was sometimes a blessing and sometimes a curse. My mixed fortune--being able to take time off and explore Oregon—sometimes got me into trouble. During that period, one of the items on my list of things to do in this lifetime was to swim out to Wizard Island in Crater Lake.

The closest campsite to the shortest route across to Wizard Island was Lightning Springs. It was important for me to get an early start the day I attempted it. Even in August, the weather can change quickly in the mountains and the swim itself would take about an hour, more or less.

The hike down and back up the rim of the lake would be a royal pain. Arriving at the parking lot and looking down the edge, I greeted a couple of sight-seers and asked if they knew what the sign that read "Stay off the **Caldera**" actually meant. They said, "No, we don't," and I really didn't think anything else of it.

Fiction in Red II

The journey down was relatively easy and only took a few minutes. The loose boulders and minor slides were inconveniences I was used to. During my considerable hunting and hiking adventures in Oregon and Washington, I had spent a considerable amount of time trekking through **shale** valleys, and I was well aware that one needs to be extremely careful on slide-prone areas and avalanche chutes.

After checking the water temperature with my hand, I made the decision to cross. I figured that if the water was this warm in the morning—pegging it at a chilly but non-life- threatening 60-something degrees, I reasoned that the afternoon temperature would be downright pleasant.

The first stop on my swim was the **emerald** pools, whose curiosity factor was one of the subscripts on my to-do list. It turned out, however, that what sounded like an idyllic spot to savor was just a couple of areas **laden** with stringy algae.

The next part of my swim was a short splash over to the main island itself, and then hike to the top, where the mini-crater was located. Spending the next few hours on and around Wizard Island was enjoyable, but it wasn't all that exciting. I met a few tourists who had splurged on one of the expensive boat tours, but they mainly stayed on the shore, fishing for trout and small Kokanee salmon.

By noon, I was getting hungry, so I decided to head back to the "mainland" a little earlier than planned. After checking to see that my shoes were still double-knotted, I jumped into the lake. As there were no rocks, I thought that I might as well go down a few extra feet deep—just for the heck of it.

Wow, what a refreshing shock! Perhaps the Indian Lore was right! Mazama was the entrance to the underworld. Or, maybe this lake was another entrance to Dante's Inferno and Cocytus was giving up some of it's icy heat! It turned out that only the top couple feet of water was warm. The **thermal stratification** band below was somewhere between 38 and 48 degrees F. I made a chilling mental note to stay on top of the first circle of hell, and then proceeded on my slow journey across the lake until I reached the other side.

Starting up the rim on foot, I stayed close to the treeline, which turned out to be a good thing, too. A slide was starting to make its way down, or so I thought. A couple of boulders the size of small televisions were headed down the hill. The sound of the cracks and direct hits of the boulders gave me time to think. They were picking up speed and gaining company, but I kept my head. I figured I should still take my time and simply be careful not to trip on the rock slide. I headed over to the biggest tree, using my hands to steady my progress. I said to myself that there is no place for style when you are trying to save your skin. Making it to the tree that had a three-foot diameter, I was able to stay away from the boulders that continued on their way, rolling around both sides of the tree.

Slides do stop, I thought. And I do not.

Fiction in Red II

When I reached the parking lot, I was more than a little surprised to find one Oregon State Patrol car blocking the back of my station wagon, and two park ranger patrol cars on either side. Noting that there were no other cars in one of the most popular viewpoints parking lots, I reasoned I was in trouble for swimming out to the island. I was wrong; I was in trouble for walking down the Caldera. It turned out that a man had slipped to his death there, a few weeks earlier.

All I could say in response to the **interrogation** was, "Yes, sir. No, sir. I didn't know, sir," until the Oregon State Patrol officer surveyed the others in attendance, and said, "Gentlemen, there is absolutely no need for me to take this guy into custody. I have to leave."

Looking rather **perturbed**, the Park Rangers handed me a piece of paper documenting my $5,000 dollar fine, and let me go. The actual violation, it turned out, was devised in an attempt to protect the fragile ecosystem of the rim of the lake and down to the water's edge, not to mention the injuries and deaths that have occurred over the years. Swimming in the lake, the officers informed me, was OK, but the only legal access to the lake was the Cleetwood Cove Trail on the other side of the lake.

Under the circumstances, I decided I might as well drive over to Rim Village and order one of the Crater Lake gift shop's world-famous ice cream cones. As I walked over to the viewing area, I struck up a conversation with a guy who was also savoring a vanilla cone, and the subject of the island came up. He asked, "Were you here an hour ago when everyone came running out of the gift shop when someone announced that a person was swimming out in the middle of the lake?"

Being unable to suppress my laughter, I extracted my $5,000 dollar ticket from my pocket, and said, "Well, no, because I was the guy in the lake!" He didn't believe me at first, until I produced my "lifetime to-do" list—and showed him the line I'd crossed through the No. 7 entry: Swim out to Wizard Island.

"Well, son, I hope it was worth it," he replied, to which I replied, "Someday it will be, I'm sure."

About 18 months later I had the good fortune to be accidentally offered a job with the vending concessionaire at the Crater Lake cafeteria. One of the standard requirements for all new hires was to attend, within a few days of being hired, the standard "Crater Lake safety talk" put on by a couple of park rangers. The three new hires, myself included, were told that the "orientation" would take about an hour, and was mandatory.

It was a pretty standard talk until the part when we were told not to walk on the Caldera. At that point, I piped up that nobody knows what a Caldera is, and therefore, all of the signs around the lake should be changed. Fortunately or unfortunately, the head park ranger was there that day, and he spoke up.

Fiction in Red II

"Our job here is to educate people," he replied stiffly. I replied, "So how does it feel to be a murderer? Nobody cares or knows what a Caldera is when they are here on vacation; all they care about is enjoying the scenery." I further ventured that if the park posted signs that read, "Please do not walk on the rim," and also posted the stiff fine, that might save quite a few lives over the years.

While the ranger stammered to come back with an **adequate** response, I said, "It takes a really big man to admit he's wrong, and the next time someone falls to their death, I don't want to be the one to ask what else I could have done to prevent it."

Witnessing my **resolve** to refuse to back down," he contritely replied, "I'll look into it."

The signs were changed within the week.

Moral of all of these Stories: Know your vocabulary!

NOTES

NOTES

NOTES

NOTES